Caelen's Wife

Book Two

A Whisper of Fate

by

Suzan Tisdale

For Kitty H. and Ophelia H.

Suzan Tisdale

Caelen's Wife - <u>A Whisper of Fate</u> is book two of a three part novel. It does end in a cliff hanger. The third book <u>A Breath of Promise</u> will be availalbe March 27, 2015.

Suzan Tisdale

Prologue

Caelen reaffirmed his declaration with a kiss.

'Twas sweet at first. Soft, tender, just a whisper of a kiss.

Fiona's knees practically knocked together.

With great care, he placed a large hand at the small of her back and with the other, he cupped her cheek, and ever so gently he pulled her closer. He'd garner no complaint from her.

Then the kiss turned from something sweet and tender to heated and passionate. Heat, from his body or hers, or both, either way, it felt much like when a fresh log is added to the hearth; a quiet *swoosh* just before bursting into flames.

'Twas a promise of things that could happen if she allowed the kiss to progress. At the moment she did not have the wherewithal to tell him to stop. She found she rather liked the way her stomach tingled and tightened and the way her toes tickled.

His tongue traced along the gap between her lips, demanding entry. Deciding she did not want the kiss to end, she gave passage. She sucked in a deep breath when the tip of his tongue touched hers. Her skin turned to gooseflesh and that odd, tingling sensation moved from her stomach to parts of her she hadn't been aware she owned until that moment.

James had never kissed her like this, with such wanton abandon. James had never made her feel so alive and excited.

James.

Oh, no, this would not work!

No matter how alive and utterly female she felt at the moment, she had to stop before things went as far as she so desperately wanted them to.

Taking a deep breath, she placed her palms against Caelen's chest and pulled away from his glorious and magnificent mouth.

"Please, stop," she said as she gasped for air.

She could not quite describe the smile he offered her. 'Twas a combination of deviousness and pride. He gave a slow shake of his head. "I do no' think ye truly wish fer me to stop. I ken that I do no' wish to."

How was she to respond to that? 'Twas only the truth he spoke. Truly, she had no desire for him to cease. If anything, she wanted to let her drying cloth fall to the floor and then have him carry her to that very warm-looking and rather inviting bed that was just a step or two away.

Nay! She had to be strong, had to put her foot down and had to behave like a logical thinking woman. She could not give in.

Her eyes soaked in all of him. Those dark brown eyes of his sparkled with what could only be described as desire. And those lips ... she had tasted those lips and knew all too well how they could make her feel. Her eyes fell to his chest. She had felt that hard-as-stone chest pressed against her own and wondered what he might look like sans the light blue tunic he now wore.

"Do ye truly wish me to stop, Fiona?" Caelen asked. His voice was soft, his tone sincere.

Did she? Did she *truly* want this to end here? Now?

Yer a woman full grown for heaven's sake! Yer a widow, no' some innocent, calf-eyed lass with delusions of grandeur or illusions of a lifetime of moments like these. There are no more moments like this in yer future. 'Tis now or never, Fiona McPherson.

She swallowed once, then again, before answering. "Nay, Caelen, I do no' wish fer ye to stop."

One

'Twas true that Fiona did not want him to stop.

Promises of untold pleasures could be found in those sparkling brown eyes of his. She hoped Caelen could not hear her thundering heart as it beat against her breast, or that he would not notice the way her body quaked with uncertainty.

Caelen did not give her any time in which to change her mind. Wrapping his big hands around her waist, he pulled her closer. His lips felt hot yet soft against hers, making her breaths jagged and harsh. She clung to him, fighting to keep from falling apart in his arms.

Countless new sensations tickled her inside to out, turning her skin to gooseflesh. His calloused hands turned to silk as his fingertips trailed up her back and down again. Breathing became increasingly difficult; thinking any coherent thought impossible.

His lips left hers, leaving her breathless and wanting. He left trails of heat behind with those glorious, magnificent lips, from her cheek, down her neck, to that very tender spot behind her ear.

Nay, it had never felt like this with James. James had never taken his time like this with hot tender kisses, soft caresses. Nay, joining with James had never taken much time. There'd been no careful exploration of her body; it had simply been a man doing his duty, trying to get his wife with child, nothing more. Afterwards, she'd always felt ashamed, severely lacking on so many levels, and broken.

This, this was entirely different. Exhilarating, wondrous and intoxicating.

Still, doubts crept in. Mayhap she should warn him now, before he got far too excited, before *she* became far too excited and they both ended up disappointed.

"Caelen," she whispered, not recognizing her own voice.

"Hmmm?" he hummed against her neck as his fingertips gently touched her shoulders.

"I," she needed to tell him something, but couldn't remember once his fingertips found their way to her breasts. Oh, she could not think when he did that. But there was something she needed to tell him. Something important.

His attentions turned to the other side of her neck then, his fingers dancing tenderly across her skin. Good Lord she was going to faint soon, she just knew it. And what was she doing just standing there? Shouldn't she be kissing him? Touching him? Her mind was a jumbled, incoherent mess.

Ever so tenderly, he took her hands in his and placed sweet kisses on each of her fingertips before he started to pull her toward the bed. The bed. The big, empty, inviting bed. A flood of depressing memories came crashing in then, pulling her out of her stupor.

"Wait!" she cried out as she pulled her hands away from his.

Caelen stared at her with a most confused expression. "Have ye changed yer mind?" he asked, looking as though he was praying she hadn't.

"Nay," she said, swallowing hard and doing her best to get her breathing back under control.

He let out the breath he'd been holding as a smile erupted on his face. "Good," he said happily. "Fer I fear the loch be nowhere cold enough to quench me desire fer ye."

When he took a step toward her, she jumped back and held up one hand. "Wait!"

He stopped, held his hands up in defeat. "What be the matter, Fiona?"

"I need to tell ye somethin'," she said as she looked around for her drying cloth. It was on the floor by Caelen's feet. "I need the dryin' cloth," she said, indicating with her head the spot near his feet.

"Why?" he asked with a raised brow.

"Because I be naked," she said, covering her breasts with her arms.

His smile turned quite devious. "I like ye that way."

"But I have to tell ye somethin', and I would prefer no' to tell ye whilst I be naked."

He sighed, scooped up the drying cloth and stepped toward her. Again, she jumped back and away as if he was a dangerous animal. Mayhap he was.

"Fiona, please, lass, ye can tell me anythin'," he said as he stretched out his arm and offered her the cloth. "Naked or fully clothed, ye can tell me anythin'."

Oh, how she prayed he meant what he said. She took the cloth and wrapped it tightly around her shoulders. It didn't help her unease. She stared at him, suddenly wishing for a place to hide, to run, to avoid the embarrassment she was about to face. Mayhap he would be kind and not laugh at her. She couldn't bear to have him laugh at her.

He waited. And he waited. And he waited. Finally, he blew out a long breath and sat on the edge of the bed. "What is it ye wanted to tell me?"

Fiona cleared her throat and took a fortifying breath. "May I please have yer promise that ye'll no' yell at me, or worse yet, laugh?"

His brows furrowed as he cocked his head to one side. "Aye, I do so promise."

"If ye yell or laugh, so help me Caelen, I'll run ye through with me sword and every *sgian dubh* in me possession."

She saw a twinkle of amusement in his eyes. "I swear I will," she told him.

"I promise, I'll no' yell, laugh or do anythin' else to upset ye."

She searched his eyes again and felt he meant to keep his word. The words poured out, so quickly that even she didn't quite understand what she had said. "Me womanly parts be broken!"

He looked at her with such an odd expression that she felt as though every square inch of her skin burned with embarrassment. "Beg yer pardon?"

Frustration took hold. "Me womanly parts be broken!" she

repeated, as if that clarified everything. He continued to look puzzled. "They do no' work proper."

"At the risk of being gutted, can ye please explain what ye mean that they *do no' work proper?*"

She swallowed hard before answering. "They do no' work proper, like other women ye may have known."

Caelen sighed and shook his head. "I fear I do no' ken what ye mean, Fiona."

"I—" 'twas too humiliating to put to voice, but she knew she must. "I have never found me woman's release."

He was as still as a stone obelisk.

"That does no' mean that we can no' —" she paused, her humiliation growing by leaps and bounds. "That does no' mean that we can no', or that is to say, that you can no' enjoy me company, if ye still want to that is. I ken it can be verra frustratin' fer a man, when his woman can no', that is, when she be unable to enjoy the experience as much as he. I mean, 'twas frustratin' fer James, and after a few times, he quit tryin', but yer no' James and I really should no' be thinkin' of him now, but I felt I should warn ye, so that when I do no', ye will no' be frustrated to the point of anger." She took a deep breath, lowered her voice and her eyes. "I could no' bear that."

Before she knew it, he was standing before her, his hands on her shoulders. "Fiona, ye mean ye've never? Not once?"

Tears pooled in her eyes and she could not bear to look at him. "I think I was close once, but nay, I've no'."

When she heard him chuckle softly, her eyes and mouth flew open, her anger quite apparent. "Ye promised ye'd no' laugh!"

"Fiona, ye need no' be ashamed or embarrassed. Some women just need a little extra time to find it, is all."

She scrunched her brow and looked for signs of deception.

"And there be a number of different ways to help ye."

She didn't dare ask him for clarification. 'Twas humiliating enough to admit her defect, let alone ask him for clarification.

He leaned in and pressed a kiss to her lips. "And I'm perfectly willin' to explore all those different ways with ye."

Her stomach lurched, tightened, and grew warm. Everything about the man held a promise, from his deep, soft voice to his fingertips.

"I have me hands," he said as he carefully took a breast into each of his palms. "I have me fingers, too." He caressed and teased with his fingertips. "And I have me mouth and tongue," he said, as his mouth found hers again.

In that kiss, Fiona knew that being with Caelen would not remotely resemble anything she'd ever done with James.

Fiona woke hours later, with Caelen's arms wrapped around her and one heavy leg tossed over hers. Her head rested quite comfortably against his chest. The fur that covered the window flapped lazily, battling against the strong breeze. The warm afternoon air smelled of Bog Myrtle and bluebells and it tickled her skin. Over the soft crackle of low burning embers she could hear children laughing somewhere out of doors.

Soft steady breaths signified Caelen was in a deep sleep. His heart beat steadily and 'twas more beautiful than any bard's song she'd ever heard. His scent, a combination of smoke, leather and soap, was more intoxicating than the finest Spanish wine. Searching her memory for a time in her life when she felt this content and satisfied, she came up blank. Add *that* to the long list of things she'd never before experienced.

Letting loose a soft sigh of satisfaction and peace, she snuggled in more closely. Aye, these past few hours were the things dreams were made of. Now she understood completely what all the excitement over joining with a man was about. In the future, when the women of her clan bespoke of all the excitement, fun, and joy that could be found in a man's bed — or his floor, chair or windowsill — she'd know full well what they meant.

Och! To wake up like this each morn, or to fall asleep in his arms each night? 'Twould be a dream come true.

Reality set in the moment she allowed her mind to wander to those forbidden places of her heart. The longing she felt when she realized this would be the one and only time in her life that she would wake up next to this most amazing man was like a hard slap to her face.

Nay, she told herself. 'Twas just this once, Fiona and ye take with ye but a memory. Nothin' more than that.

She'd not feel guilty for what she'd done, for what had taken place between them. Nay, the only regret she had was knowing that it was only once.

She felt Caelen raise his head for a moment before settling back into his pillow. Hugging her tightly, he kissed the top of her head. "Fer a moment, I feared I was dreamin'."

The soft timbre of his voice broke through the silence and stabbed at her heart. She had hoped to leave before he woke. Knowing full well 'twould have been a cowardly thing to do, she remained quiet, selfishly wanting to linger for just a few moments more.

"'Twill be a great honor and privilege to wake up to ye like this each morn, Fiona."

Fiona pulled away from his embrace, sat up and looked into his eyes. He was so handsome, even with that long jagged scar that ran from his forehead to his waist. She had no idea how he'd come by it and regretted the harsh reality of knowing she'd never find out. His brown eyes sparkled with delight for a moment, until he read her face. The smile faded, replaced with confusion.

He loved her, of that there was no doubt. Caelen genuinely meant the words he'd spoken earlier, that he adored her, found her beautiful and irresistible. She would give almost anything in the world to wake up to him each morn. *Almost* anything.

Words and tears were lodged in her throat as they began a battle to see which would free themselves first. She left the bed and padded across the room to her clothes. Hurriedly, she began to dress before either the tears or words had a chance to escape.

"Fiona?" Caelen said as he left the bed. "What be the matter?"

The matter? Aye, he is as daft as he is handsome and experienced in the ways of lovin'. She couldn't manage to utter a word, could only shake her head as she pushed her arms into her under shirt.

He was beside her then with a comforting hand resting on her arm. She couldn't bear to look at him. Quickly, she pulled the tunic on then grabbed her trews.

"Fiona?" His voice remained calm, soft and low, but she found no comfort in it. "Please, lass, tell me why ye look so sad?"

The tears she had tried so valiantly to hold at bay came rushing out along with her voice. "Caelen, I canna marry ye."

He took a step back and cocked his head. "Why no'? Do ye no' love me?"

Love him? With every fiber of her being she loved him, but knew nothing could come of it. "It matters no' how I feel, Caelen. I canna marry ye," she told him as she thrust one leg into her trews, then the other. The room seemed to grow smaller with each moment that passed whilst the ache in her heart intensified.

"Do ye love me or no'?" he asked, his voice calmly demanding an honest answer.

Fiona choked back a sob and nodded her head in affirmation. "Aye, I do, Caelen, but that changes nothin'. I canna marry ye." Needing out of the room, she jumped to her feet and searched for her belt and sword, looking at everything but *him*. He was naked and she knew that a naked Caelen was far more dangerous than a fully-clothed and armed Caelen.

She located her belt on the floor next to the hearth, grabbed it and wrapped it around her waist. "I must return home," she told him, unable to concentrate on anything more than the ache in her heart.

Daggers. She needed her daggers. Finding them on the mantel she began tucking those into her boots and belt.

"Why can ye no' marry me?"

Without thinking, she answered him harshly. "I canna and will no' sacrifice me clan fer ye, or any other man, Caelen. I'll no' do that to them."

"Why must ye sacrifice yer clan to be with me? To be me wife?"

She took a step forward, rallying the courage to finally look at him. If she kept her eyes on his, she'd be able to make it out of the room with some of her dignity intact. If she lowered them to his broad, hard chest, or parts further south, she would be doomed and damned.

"If I marry ye, my clan will be absorbed into yers. I'll no' let that happen."

From his expression she knew he was silently questioning her sanity. "And what would be wrong with that?"

"I made a *vow*, Caelen, much like ye did when ye were made chief. I made a vow to protect me clan, me people at all costs. I also made a vow to James and to his father that I would never allow Clan McPherson to fall."

"And ye think that by joinin' with Clan McDunnah, it falls?"

"Aye, it means just that." All at once she felt angry, broken and miserable.

The last thing she had wanted was to leave on bad terms. But his suggestion of marriage and his inability to see how important it was to keep her clan together, irked her. She paused with her hand on the handle to the door. Speaking to him over her shoulder, she said, "Caelen, I need ye to know that today has been both the happiest and saddest day of me life." She swallowed back the tears and took a deep breath. "I do love ye, Caelen McDunnah. But I canna be with ye as yer wife or mistress, or anythin' else."

Without waiting for a response, she pulled the door open and left.

Caelen had to admire her determination to not break the vow she made to her clan. But that did not mean he would not do everything within his power to make her his wife.

Why couldn't she see the benefit of her clan joining his? He could protect her, he could protect her people. Why was that so difficult to understand?

She left him standing naked in the middle of the room, dumbfounded with her level of stubbornness. Any other woman would have jumped with unrestrained glee at becoming his wife.

But Fiona McPherson was not like any other woman.

Bloody hell.

"Fiona!" he called out to her as she stepped out into the hallway. "Wait!"

Finding his clothes scattered on the floor where he'd left them hours ago, he pulled on his trews first before heading out to stop her from leaving. His heart pounded, fearful it might lose the one woman he could say without equivocation that he loved.

Unconditionally.

Without regard to anyone or anything else.

He loved her.

Rushing out of the room, he went after the woman who had stolen his heart, and if she left, the very life from his soul.

Caelen bounded down the hallway calling out Fiona's name. He rounded the corner and slammed into a confused looking Phillip.

"Out of me way," Caelen thundered as he tried to push his way around Phillip.

"Nay," Phillip said as he grabbed Caelen's shoulders. "Let her go."

Caelen shoved Phillip aside and ran toward the stairs. Fiona was just reaching the bottom step when he called out for her again. "Fiona! Wait!"

She paused only briefly to glance at him over her shoulder.

He saw it then, the pain in her eyes as tears rolled down her cheeks. He could also see her profound determination.

Her mind was made up.

His wasn't.

Caelen started toward her until she crossed her palms over her heart and mouthed the words *I love ye*. A heartbeat later, she turned and fled.

He would not, could not accept her belief that there was no way for them to be together. Certainly they could work together to find a way. As he took another step toward the stairs, a strong hand reached out and grabbed his arm to pull him back.

"Caelen, let her go," Phillip said in a low, calm voice. "If ye love that woman, ye'll need to let her go."

"I'll do no such thing, Phillip," Caelen ground out. "And if ye value yer life, ye'll remove yer hand."

Phillip shook his head. "Ye must let her figure it out, Caelen. If ye force her to make a decision now, ye'll both regret it all the rest of yer days."

Caelen pulled his arm from Phillip's grasp. "What do ye ken of it?" he demanded.

"I ken ye love her, any fool can see it, Caelen. I've been speakin' with Brodie. She'll no' give up the helm, she'll no' break her word to her people. Fiona loves ye, but she's fightin' a battle with her heart now. Do no' make her choose between ye or her clan, lad, fer yer certain to lose."

It pained Caelen to no end when he realized Phillip was right. If he tried to force Fiona to make such a decision, he would not end the victor. But what was he to do? She was fleeing his keep as if it were on fire. How could he stop her from leaving?

"What do ye suggest I do?" Caelen asked through gritted teeth.

Phillip rested a hand on Caelen's shoulder. "Let her go. Let her come to the decision on her own."

Caelen swallowed hard, his heart slowly cracking bit by ugly bit. "And if she does no' choose me?"

Phillip smiled warmly. "She'll choose ye, Caelen. She'll choose ye."

Two

It had to have been the longest ride of her life. Fiona refused to shed a tear in front of her brother or her men. Instead, she would bottle them up and save them for after they arrived at their keep. For a time when she was alone and could wallow in her pain without an audience.

The closer they drew to her home, the more her heart shattered. She reckoned that by the time they made it home, her heart would be nothing more than tiny, miniscule pieces of dust.

Had she known in advance that it would hurt this much to leave Caelen, she never would have allowed herself to succumb to his touch. Nay, she realized that wasn't true. It had been the most enjoyable, wondrous, exciting few hours of her life and she'd not give one moment of it back just to ease her aching heart. 'Twas far better to have one moment of something quite special, than to live an entire life of nothing.

"What did Caelen do to ye, Fi?" William asked in a low voice as he rode next to her. When she did not answer, he began a slew of rushed questions. "Did he hurt ye? Did the bastard seduce ye with promises he means no' to keep? Tell me, Fi."

"William, he did no' seduce me," she told him pointedly, silently wishing he'd simply go away and leave her to her heartache.

William studied her closely, his anger growing quite evident with his set jaw and the thunderous look in his eye. "What happened, Fi? I need to ken so I can avenge yer honor!"

"Me honor does no' need avenged, William. Truthfully, 'tis none of yer concern what did or did no' happen between Caelen

20

and me." She tapped the flanks of her horse, urging it forward in an attempt to be away from her brother's interrogation.

From the day she was born, William had convinced himself he was her protector and guardian of her heart. Fiona knew he would not give up until he was convinced she was well.

"Fi," he said as he pulled his horse beside her again. "I do no' believe fer a moment that ye are well. Now tell me, what happened."

She released her frustration with a rapid sigh. "Nothin' happened," she told him. "I be simply tired, frustrated and hungry. Ye need no' concern yerself with Caelen, fer he was nothin' short of a gentleman." 'Twas a lie but she didn't care. "'Tis also time fer me courses." Another lie and again, she did not care.

Her *courses* had gotten her out of many a difficult or awkward situation over the years, especially when it came to her brothers. All she need do to either garner sympathy or get herself out of trouble was to tell them 'twas that time of the month. Instantly, any anger they held toward her fell away, for those monthly problems were a mysterious thing. Her brothers neither understood nor possessed a desire to. Some things they reckoned, were best left alone.

William's cheeks burned red as he stammered for an appropriate response. "Oh," he said quietly. "I'll leave ye be then."

From a room in the tower, Caelen watched Fiona leave with her brother William and the rest of her men. He remained there until long after she faded from sight. She had taken his heart with her, leaving him as bereft and as alone as a piece of driftwood floating through the wide ocean.

The cloak of night draped itself across the land. The evening meal came and went and the keep had settled into the quiet and still hours of night, and yet he remained looking out at the horizon.

A cool damp breeze flittered in through the tall, narrow window where he'd been acting as sentry. Stirring up tiny whirlwinds of dust at his feet, the air caressed his skin. His skin turned to gooseflesh, for the air was as soft and gentle as Fiona's whispers against his skin. Whispers of fate he might not ever get to experience again if he allowed his breaking heart to guide him now.

There simply had to be a way for them to be together, as husband and wife.

After hours of searching for a solution he made several decisions. First and most importantly, he would not take no for an answer. It had taken him sixteen years to get over the loss of his first wife and their son. He refused to spend the rest of his life mourning the loss of another woman, a woman he loved more than he could ever have thought possible.

Fiona had done something to his long-sheltered heart. With no effort on her part, she had somehow managed to get the bloody thing beating again. And he'd be damned if he'd allow circumstance or stubbornness to shatter it again.

He'd either find a way or he'd make a way to have Fiona McPherson as his wife.

Night had fallen across the land by the time Fiona, William and the others returned to their keep. While she would have preferred to crawl into bed and spend the next fortnight crying her eyes out, Fiona knew she couldn't. If she was giving up the chance at a life with Caelen because she was chief then she needed to behave as one. She would deal with her emotions later.

Pushing aside the ache in her heart, she and William met with Collin and her advisors in her private study. Collin and the others let out a collective sigh of relief at learning she hadn't done anything foolish — such as cutting Caelen's throat.

Collin and William sat on either side of her at the long table, while Andrew, Seamus, and Richard took up seats opposite them. With a calmness that belied her crushed heart, Fiona explained what they had learned from Brodie.

"So ye no longer believe the McDunnahs be responsible fer the attacks?" Richard asked quite pointedly.

"Aye," Fiona answered. "I believe there be someone who wants to make it appear as though the McDunnahs are to blame. Though why, I canna say at the moment. There has to be more to it than someone wantin' magical water."

"Who kens what makes any man do anythin'?" Andrew asked rhetorically. "It verra well could be somethin' as simple as that."

All eyes then focused on Andrew. "We've been somewhat isolated here all these many years," he began, "but we all ken that

22

evil exists. If a man were to believe that McPherson water holds magical powers, he might verra well be moved to do whatever he must to have it. He needs no other reason than his belief that he can somehow benefit from it. Whether it be a financial benefit or somethin' else."

While Fiona found it difficult to believe anyone could be moved to murder over supposed magical water, she knew Andrew was right. Some men could be motivated by nearly anything. Still, doubts lingered. "Ye may verra well be right, Andrew. Still, me instinct tells me there be far more to it than that."

"Be that as it may," Richard chimed in. "What do we do now? Ye've got four clan chiefs due here on the morrow. What do ye plan to tell them?"

Fiona had forgotten about the summit she had called for after Bridgett's death. "We meet with them," she answered. "Mayhap we'll be able to learn who is truly behind this."

"So it be no longer a war summit?" Richard asked, as he tried to hide his disappointment. Of all the people in the room, Richard was perhaps the only one who actually looked forward to the prospect of war. Ornery and at times short tempered, Richard was never one to back down from anything. Inwardly, Fiona chuckled. *And they worry over me startin' a war?*

"Nay," Fiona told him. "No longer a war summit. 'Twill be more a mission to learn the truth, or at least part of it."

"I pray yer right," Andrew said. "At this point, I'm less concerned over the *why* of it than the *who*."

Richard smiled at Andrew. "I agree, Andrew. And if it be all right with the rest of ye, I'd like to be the one who guts the bloody bastard responsible fer takin' our Bridgett."

Fiona could not argue with Richard's desire for retribution. "I imagine, Richard, that we will all be wantin' a piece of him."

Richard laughed loudly. "Aye, by the time we're all done with him, I doubt there'll be much left fer even the bugs to feast upon.

Three

Answers could not be found amongst the men who had proposed to Fiona. Usually rumors flew across the Highlands as fast as a rabbit could run. But this time? People simply weren't talking.

Mayhap the troubles were not coming from the chiefs who had proposed, but from someone else. Caelen did not believe in coincidences. However, at this point he did not have the luxury of ruling out the possibility that the proposals and raids were not linked.

If he could not find the answers here, then he would have to expand his search.

He would begin by enlisting the help of Angus McKenna, chief of the Clan MacDougall.

There was little time to spare. Caelen sent a messenger to Angus McKenna to give advance warning of his arrival. He didn't bother seeking permission to visit MacDougall lands, for it was neither in his nature to ask nor was it necessary. Caelen also sent a message to his oldest and closest friend, Nial McKee.

Though Angus was only twelve years his senior, Caelen still thought of him as the father he'd never had. Aye, Caelen may have sprung from Nerbert McDunnah's loins, but that was as far as the connection to the man went.

The MacDougalls and McDunnahs had been allies for many years, but their relationship went beyond more than just a political alignment. Not only were the chiefs of each clan good friends, many friendships and even a few marriages, had been forged between the clanspeople.

In addition to those friendships, the MacDougalls and McDunnahs were the leading parties in a hopefully irrevocable agreement referred to as *The Bond of The Seven*. The bond was forged years ago between their two clans and the Grahams, McKees, Carruthers, Lindsays and Randolphs. If ever any of them were in dire need of assistance, all they need do is send out the call.

He had just finished giving last minute orders to Kenneth when one of the younger lads entered the gathering room.

"Caelen," the boy said. He was out of breath and looked pensive. "Yer grandminny sends fer ye. She says it be important."

Caelen blew out a frustrated breath, thanked the lad and sent him off to tell Burunild he'd be there momentarily.

"Would ye like to go as a witness?" Caelen asked Kenneth.

"Witness to what?"

"Fer when they ask why I strangled the auld woman ye can tell them because she drove me to it." Caelen replied. "The woman sorely tests me."

Kenneth chuckled as he rubbed his bearded jaw. "Aye, she can be a trial at times."

Caelen looked aghast. "At times?" he asked. "The only time she's no' testin' me is when she be asleep."

Kenneth continued to chuckle, enjoying his cousin's discomfit. "What? That wee, sweet auld woman? She's as kind and generous as the day is long, cousin."

"Then *ye* go see what she wants. I'd rather do battle against a horde of angry Huns."

"Nay, ye need to see her. God only kens how much time the woman has left to grace His earth."

Caelen rolled his eyes and held up his hands in defeat. "So she's been tellin' me fer the last thirty years of me life."

Burunild made no attempt to hide her disappointment in Caelen. "What do ye mean she's left? Ye promised I could meet the warrior woman!"

Caelen thought his grandminny was behaving like a spoilt child. He swallowed back the urge to tell her just that. "Grandminny, I ken what I told ye, but she would no' stay." He couldn't bear to tell her the truth, that Fiona had turned down his offer of marriage and left him a broken man.

"But why?" Burunild asked as she banged her walking stick against the stone floor.

Caelen's head began to ache from lack of sleep, from his broken heart and his frustrating grandminny. Rubbing his temples with his fingers, he tried to find the words to explain without telling her the truth. "She was verra busy and had important things to attend to."

"Will she come back?" Burunild asked with a furrowed brow, as if she were waiting to catch him in a lie.

"I can only pray that she does," he murmured.

Burunild sat back in her chair and studied him closely for several long moments.

"Grandminny," Caelen said, and even he thought his voice sounded tired. "I be leavin' this morn. I leave Phillip behind. He'll see to it that yer taken care of in me stead." He let out a tired breath and stood.

"Ye love her, don' ye?" Burunild asked.

Caelen stared down at the auld woman. Her concern seemed genuine, but experience told him that his grandminny couldn't be trusted. She wasn't truly an evil woman, just an auld woman who didn't want to be ignored or set aside as if she were too stupid or senile to be of use to anyone. However, she oft used her age to her advantage and there were many times when he was quite certain her goal in life was to make him as miserable as possible. She was a paradox, this auld woman.

"This warrior woman," Burunild said, craning her neck to look up at her grandson. "Ye love her."

There was no way around it. The auld woman would hound him to death until he answered. "Aye, Grandminny, I fear I do."

Something flickered in her aged, watery eyes. Something Caelen could not quite describe. Was it a grandmother's adoration? Humor? Or something else he thought he should be quite afraid of.

Burunild nodded her head as if everything in the world made sense, placed her hands on the top of her table and stood to look at Caelen. "Well, it be about time."

Caelen looked heavenward for patience for he knew he was about to be the recipient of one of his grandminny's lectures.

"I be verra happy fer ye, grandson, that ye've finally found true love."

Uncertain if 'twas a ruse he remained quiet, his brow knotted by puzzlement.

"Fer sixteen years, ye mourned the death of a woman ye did no' truly love. Aye, ye loved her, but no' like ye love this woman. I can see it in yer eyes, hear it in yer voice." She studied him closely for a moment. "Fer the first time in yer life, ye've gotten a glimpse at *true* love, grandson. But I fear ye be on the brink of losin' it. Ye must fight fer the woman, fer I promise ye, the heartache from losin' yer first Fiona be only a glimpse at the pain ye'll endure if ye lose this one."

A sadness fell over her then. Caelen didn't think it possible for her to look aulder or more tired, but when her shoulders sagged and the twinkle left her eyes ... he knew in that wee moment that his grandminny knew from harsh experience exactly of what she spoke. Just under the surface of her wrinkled, at times severe exterior, lay a broken heart. It nearly buckled his knees to think of his grandminny living through the hell he was now living.

"'Tis a heartache unlike any other, Caelen. One ye might survive but ye never truly heal from. Do no' let this woman get away from ye, lad. Fer I fear ye won't live long enough to regret it."

With his messengers sent Caelen, Kenneth and twenty of their finest men set off for MacDougall lands just after dawn. Barring any unforeseen problems or bad weather, they would reach the MacDougall keep by nightfall on the following day.

"What do ye hope to gain by visitin' with the MacDougall?" Kenneth asked as he rode alongside Caelen.

"'Tis more than a visit, Kenneth. I hope to enlist his help in findin' out who is behind the attacks on Fiona's people."

With one curious brow raised, Kenneth said, "So she be *Fiona* now, aye?"

Caelen shot an angry glance toward his cousin. He was in a foul mood and would not brook any teasing or meddling from anyone, least of all his cousin.

"And what, pray tell, do ye plan to do if we learn who is truly behind the attacks on the McPhersons?"

"I plan on killin' the bloody bastard."

That seemed to please Kenneth, for he was almost as bloodthirsty as Caelen. "And if ye do no' find the answers ye seek with the aid of the MacDougalls?"

"I'll search this world over, to find out who is tryin' to make me look like a reiver of sheep and a murderer," Caelen told him bluntly. He had no qualms in doing just that. Not only was his honor, as well as the clan's, at stake, Fiona's life could be in danger as well.

Some time passed, as they rode along the countryside, before Kenneth spoke again. "Tell me, Caelen, what is it about this woman that has ye in such a state?"

Caelen was unaware of being in any 'state' other than furious and told Kenneth just that. "The only 'state' I be in is angry, fer I do no' like bein' tested or made a fool."

"Be it the bonny Fiona who is testin' ye? Has she made a fool out of ye?"

Caelen was about three heartbeats away from wiping the smirk from Kenneth's bearded face.

"Fiona has done nothin' wrong, Kenneth. And I'll warn ye to tread lightly on that subject, or avoid it altogether. Fer I'll no' think twice about poundin' yer ugly face into the ground."

'Twas true that Fiona was not to blame for his current mood. Aye, he was angry that she had refused to even consider his proposal. But he was much more angry about the situation they'd been thrown into by some unknown force.

"She be a bonny woman, Caelen, and right fierce," Kenneth remarked. "I be only curious as to what it is about this particular woman who has stolen yer heart — a heart that I did no' know ye even possessed until these past few days."

Instead of telling Kenneth the truth — that he was just as confused over the entire situation as he — he said, "Shut up, Kenneth."

His stern look and harsh tone apparently meant nothing to Kenneth.

"I only be curious, Caelen."

He sounded sincere, but Caelen was not about to share his innermost feelings with Kenneth, at least not as they pertained to Fiona McPherson.

"Ye'll get no further warnin', Kenneth. The next time ye open yer mouth I will shut it fer ye," Caelen warned him through gritted teeth. Not waiting for a response, Caelen kicked the flanks of his horse and rode to the front of the line, leaving his cousin behind him.

Four

One by one, the chiefs from clans McKenzie, Farquar, McGregor, MacElroy and MacKinnon, began to pour into the McPherson keep. Whilst William and Seamus greeted each man at the gates, Collin met them at the door and led them into the gathering room.

Fiona decided to wait until the last man arrived before making an appearance. She saw no reason to repeat her intentions again and again. 'Twas best to address them all at once.

She was not looking forward to meeting with these men. With her hands clasped behind her back, she paced to and fro, betwixt her hearth and her desk and thought on the events of the past weeks. If she ever got her hands on the man responsible for turning her life into its current unrecognizable state, she'd filet him like a salmon and leave his innards for the scavengers.

The room grew uncomfortably small and hot as she paced back and forth. Her trews, which usually made her feel quite confident and comfortable, itched and scratched against her skin. Her mail which normally felt as light as a feather began to weigh her down, feeling as if 'twere made of stone. Even her boots felt awkward.

"Calm yerself, Fiona McPherson," she muttered under her breath. "Ye've nothin' to fear this day. Ye be the chief of yer clan no' some innocent wee bairn."

Suddenly, she wished her mother and father were here if only to offer sage advice. There was not a day that went by that she didn't think of them, though in truth, she was much closer to her father than her mother.

'Twasn't as if she liked one more than the other. Nay, she loved both her parents. They were good, decent people. She simply had more in common with her father. He understood her passion for the blade, for needing to feel capable and strong. Her mum, however, would quietly shake her head in dismay and encourage Fiona to take on more lady-like endeavors.

Fiona was so lost in her own thoughts that she hadn't heard Mairi enter the study. "Fi," Mairi said as she balanced her seven-month-old son Symon on her hip. "William sends word that the MacKinnon has just entered McPherson lands. He should be here within the hour."

"Thank ye, Mairi," Fiona said, smiling when she saw wee Symon. He was chewing ferociously on a long strip of untanned leather while drool ran down his chin. He looked quite happy at the moment, so cherubic and sweet.

"He looks in fine spirits this day," Fiona remarked as she stepped forward and caressed his cheek.

Mairi nodded as she kissed the top of Symon's bald head. "Aye, he is," Mairi said. Looking back at Fiona she said, "Fi, I never thanked ye fer helpin' us that day, fer lettin' me and Collin get some sleep after all those nights of Symon no' sleepin'."

"Think nothin' of it, Mairi. 'Twas me pleasure to spend time with me nephew."

"Ye were right, that he was cuttin' teeth and no' spoiled like me mum had convinced me," Mairi said, looking embarrassed at admitting such a thing.

Fiona decided to be diplomatic by remaining mute on the subject of Mairi's mum. Instead, she kissed the top of Symon's head before stepping away.

Mairi remained near the door, looking as though she had something more on her mind but was afraid to speak it.

"Be there somethin' else, Mairi?"

Mairi started to speak but stopped. Fiona gathered 'twas a difficult subject she needed to discuss.

"Go ahead, Mairi," Fiona said as she sat in her chair behind her desk. "We've known each other a verra long time. Ye can talk to me about anythin'."

Fiona doubted that the subject Mairi wanted to discuss was as serious as the young woman's expression indicated. Until Mairi finally spoke.

"Why do ye no' remarry, Fi? Is it because ye canna have bairns of yer own and ye fear no man would want ye because of it?"

The slightest breeze could have knocked Fiona out of her chair, so stunned was she. While she considered Mairi a good friend, a dear sister-in-law, she'd not been quite as close to the woman as she had been with Bridgett. Still, she had never discussed her barrenness with anyone, not even her long dead husband, James. It was far too difficult to think about, let alone discuss aloud.

"Fi, I did no' mean to embarrass ye or hurt yer feelin's," Mairi began as she took a step toward Fiona. "Ye are such a bonny woman, Fi and ye have so much to offer. I worry over ye, Fi, and ye seem so sad these past few days."

Fiona cleared the knot from her throat and pretended to not be upset with Mairi's question. 'Twasn't anger that she felt, but a deep sense of sadness. For the life of her, she could not figure out why Mairi had asked such a thoroughly personal question.

"Nay, Mairi, I do no' worry over it. And it be Bridgett's death that has me so melancholy." Her answer was half truth, half lie, and incomplete.

Aye, there had been a time when she worried some men would not be interested in marrying her, but not simply because she was barren. There were too many reasons to mention and now, 'twas all moot for there was a man who wanted to marry her. It was also true that Bridgett's death had a profound effect on her heart.

Mairi looked as though she did not believe Fiona's answer, but thankfully, let the matter drop.

"I shall have more refreshments taken to the gatherin' room. I'll send word when the MacKinnon has reached the gates."

Fiona managed a nod and murmur of thanks before turning her attention to unimportant scrolls splayed atop her desk. After the door closed, she let loose the breath she'd been holding.

Why had Mairi asked that particular question? And today of all days? Mayhap she was simply reaching out, trying to be a friend and sister now that Bridgett was gone.

Fiona had always held her sisters-in-law at arm's length. In truth, she did that with all women, save for Bridgett. She was by no means rude or unkind with other women, she simply felt uncomfortable around them, as if she didn't truly belong amongst them. 'Twould most likely take a lifetime of soul-searching to reason the *why* of it out. The answer, she believed, probably wasn't worth the bother.

Fiona had asked Collin to take the clan chiefs into the war room - the very same room that each of the men had proposed to her at one time or another over the past year. Once she had received word that all the men were assembled, Fiona entered.

The five chiefs sat around the table, along with Collin, Seamus, and Andrew. William and Richard stood as sentries just outside the door. Each of the chiefs had been allowed to bring no more than two men inside for the meeting, to act either as guard or advisor.

As soon as she entered, she wished she had told Collin to throw each man into the loch, along with a jar of soap, before allowing them entry. Apparently, not all of the men were as keen on cleanliness as others. The room smelled of sweat, ale, and smoke as well as an overpowering aroma of sandalwood.

Fiona paused momentarily to assess the demeanor of each man. The McGregor and Farquar looked bored, the McKenzie was half asleep, and the MacElroy looked his usual arrogant self. Only the MacKinnon seemed interested in the proceedings.

She headed toward her place at the head of the table. As she strolled past the men, she discovered the McGregor was the owner of the foul odor that lingered in the air. And MacElroy the Arrogant as she'd come to call him, had apparently bathed in sandalwood and roses, the pungent aroma making her head hurt as she walked past him. Later, she would have to thank Collin for placing those two men furthest away from her seat.

She stood at the head of the table, rested one hand on the hilt of her sword and looked out at the men before her. One, if not more, was an enemy. The person behind the raids. The person responsible for Bridgett's death.

After giving each man a nod of recognition, Fiona began. "I thank ye all fer bein' here this day."

"Before ye continue, I shall have ye know that I'm no' here to lend me support in your call to war against the McDunnah." 'Twas the McGregor who spoke. Moments ago, he looked bored. Now, he looked derisive.

The Farquar nodded in agreement. "Aye, to go against the

McDunnah is suicide."

"I have to agree," MacElroy the Arrogant chimed in. "Everyone kens that Caelen McDunnah is more than just a wee tetched."

"Gentlemen," Fiona said calmly, trying to break through the growing opinions as they pertained to Caelen.

The McGregor chuckled his consensus, and added, "*More* than just a wee tetched! The man be insane."

"Gentlemen," Fiona repeated, a little more loudly this time.

"If I've a desire to end me own life," the Farquar said, "I'll do it at the end of me own rope, not be slaughtered by those animals."

By animals, Fiona could only assume he meant the McDunnahs. Weeks ago, she might have agreed with that description. But she had come to know Caelen and some of his people. While they might be a wee rough around the edges, blunt, and lacking in finer social graces, they were good people. Not animals.

Fiona glanced down the table at Collin, Seamus, and Andrew. Andrew shrugged his shoulders as if to say *how can ye stop them?* Seamus shook his head in disgust at the rude way the men were behaving. Collin raised a brow and started to stand, but Fiona held him off with a raised palm. She needed to be the one to bring this meeting under control.

"One," she said rather loudly. "Two," she paused briefly as she caught the MacElroy's attention. "Three."

The color drained from the MacElroy's face. "Are ye countin'?" he asked with an unsteady voice.

"Aye, I am," she said as she pulled two *sgian dubhs* from her belt. "Four," she said as she tested the weight of the small blades in her hands.

"Quiet, ye bloody fools!" the MacElroy barked at the other men. "Can ye no' hear that she's countin'?"

There wasn't a man among them — save, mayhap for the man standing behind the McGregor that she did not recognize — that didn't possess firsthand experience with just how good Fiona McPherson was with a knife. Or sword or bow and arrow.

In truth Fiona would much prefer to settle any disputes like a level-headed adult. But there were times, far too many times, that words would not work, and some form or display of violence or physical strength was necessary. As long as the men before her knew she was not above using physical force, she could get them to at least listen.

Scanning the curious if not dread-filled eyes of the men, she waited until she had their full attention.

"While it be true that I had originally called ye all here to wage war against the McDunnah, I now have evidence that he was no' behind the raids." She paused briefly for her words to sink in, carefully resting the *sgian dubhs* on the table before her. "I'll no' be warrin' with them."

Their astonishment was quite apparent.

"What evidence?" the McGregor barked. "Ye call us here for war then change yer mind?"

"Just like a woman," MacElroy the Arrogant whispered.

Fiona heard him. Tempted as she was to hurl her *sgian dubhs* into his pompous heart, she resisted. "I've only just been made aware of the evidence," Fiona said, directing her statement toward MacElroy.

"Then why are we here?" the Farquar asked bewildered and confused. "I thought we were goin' to war?"

"Well, she's apparently changed her mind," the McGregor explained. "I'm just as confused as the rest of ye."

"If ye'd close yer mouths and open yer ears," Fiona said, raising her voice above the din, "ye might just learn somethin'." That had been one of her mother's favorite sayings when Fiona and her brothers were younger. It seemed befitting to use it now, since these men were behaving like children.

They turned their focus back to her and 'twas all she could do not to roll her eyes. "As I said, I've only recently been made aware of evidence that exonerates the McDunnah. He is no' the one responsible fer the raids or fer Bridgett McPherson's death." Fiona had to clear her throat to clear the knot that formed at the mention of her dearest friend. "Caelen McDunnah is innocent."

"What proof do ye have of his innocence?" the MacElroy asked. "Did ye no' declare that ye'd seen the man with yer own eyes? Were McDunnah daggers no' left behind?" he said with a disapproving shake of his head.

Fiona was prepared to give just enough information, hopefully enough that one of them might trip on his own lying tongue. "Me brother, Brodie, was with the McDunnah the night Bridgett was killed."

"That still does no' make the man innocent," the MacElroy replied. "He could be directin' his men to do his dirty work for him."

"At one point, MacElroy, I was led to believe the same," Fiona told him. "I have met with the McDunnah several times over the past weeks. He's no' the one responsible. Instead, I claim to ye that someone else be responsible, someone who wishes us all to believe it be the McDunnah. For some reason, they want us at war with him and his."

She took in a breath and waited for the men to consider her words. "I do no' ken the why of it just yet, but I will find out who is behind it all, on that, ye have me word."

Each of these men had known Fiona long enough and hopefully well enough to know that she did not make idle threats. Nor was she one who easily jumped to conclusions or judgment.

"I tell each of ye now, that I'll no' be warrin' with the McDunnah. He and I have come to a truce and I now consider him me ally."

Her last statement was meant to serve as warning. The McDunnahs were now her allies. She could only hope that the news would stop the raids.

"Though we will no' be warrin' with the McDunnah, I still need yer aid."

More confused than before, the men sat with raised brows or mouths agape.

"Aid?" The McGregor asked. "Need I remind ye that ye turned down me previous offer of aid and protection? Ye turned all of us down."

With an inward sigh, Fiona answered. "I do no' seek yer protection, McGregor, just yer aid."

The man shook his head in dismay. "Yer no' makin' much sense, McPherson."

I'd make more sense if ye'd just be quiet and let me finish. "I do no' need anyone's protection. But I would ask fer yer help in findin' out who is truly behind the raids and Bridgett's death."

The task of watching each of the chiefs carefully was up to Collin, Andrew and Seamus. Fiona, too, was studying each man intently, looking for any sign as to who the guilty party could be.

Brodie believed the McGregor was behind the raids and Fiona wasn't so certain he was wrong. The McGregor had been the first to propose, but still, she needed far more proof than her gut instinct. She needed facts.

"Are ye accusin' one of us?" the McGregor asked, clearly insulted.

"Nay," Fiona said with a shake of her head. "I do no' believe it be any one of ye here today. That be why I ask fer yer help. All I seek is information." 'Twas a lie, but a necessary one. Her gut told her that there was someone inside this room who was the true culprit, the true murderer. If she allowed them to believe she thought them all innocent, one of them might show his hand.

"If any of ye has now or comes to have any information as it pertains to the raids and Bridgett's murder, I would appreciate ye lettin' me know," she told them as she began tucking her *sgian dubhs* back into her belt.

"What is in it fer us?" the Farquar asked. He was well known for his greed, as well as being a gossip.

"Two barrels of fine McPherson whisky as well as me thanks," Fiona told him.

She cast another glance around the table, hoping for the slightest indication of guilt.

Nothing.

"The hour grows late and ye've travelled far. I welcome each of ye to join us fer our evenin' meal. Until then, ye are welcome to walk about the keep and lands if ye'd like, or take a respite in the men's solar. Collin and Seamus shall lead the way."

Without waiting for a response or indication as to what they might plan, Fiona left the men alone with the hope that Collin or one of her other men might learn something useful. For now, she needed to step out of doors for some much needed fresh air.

A light mist clung to the late afternoon air, cooling Fiona's heated cheeks. Standing at the bottom of the steps that led into the keep, Fiona took in several deep cleansing breaths. 'Twould take more than fresh air to remove the stench of the foul air that had filled her war room, mayhap even more than one bath.

The courtyard was bustling with people, mostly men that had travelled with their chiefs from the neighboring clans. Over the clatter of people talking, men boasting and guffawing, and the general commotion of daily life, she could hear the lowing of cattle coming from the pasture. Instantly, she thought of Caelen and how deeply she missed him. She imagined she could live ten lifetimes over and never stop loving the man, or missing him to the point of tears.

The ache in her heart was raw and fresh, blending with the guilt she felt at having joined with him, only to leave. The image of Caelen's face flashed in her mind's eye as she remembered the pain she had seen in his eyes when she had left. There had been no intent on her part to cause him one moment of suffering or discomfit. She'd been selfish to think that she could take what his body could offer without also taking his heart.

Did men not do that all the time? Join with a woman without regard to her heart or tender feelings? How many times had she consoled a friend or woman who had had her heart broken from those very actions and cursed the man who had left them so despondent?

Fiona took in a deep breath and let it out slowly. She had treated Caelen in precisely the same manner. She was no better than the men she had once cursed and damned to the devil.

The only way she could begin to set things right with Caelen — aside from marrying him — was to find out who was behind the raids and Bridgett's murder. She needed to prove to the rest of the world, what she already knew in her heart, that Caelen was innocent.

Frustrated that she hadn't learned anything new from her meeting with the clan chiefs, she decided to take a walk around the keep. She hadn't taken but a few steps when she heard Edgar MacKinnon's deep voice calling her name.

"Fiona," he said as he bounded down the steps.

She paused and waited for him to catch up. When he reached her, he offered a smile and a nod. "I wonder," he said, "if ye might have time to discuss what just happened."

Fiona trusted Edgar MacKinnon as much as the other clan chiefs — not one bit. "Aye, I do, if ye do no' mind takin' a wee walk."

Another smile from the small man's thin lips. Shorter than Fiona by a good two inches, his thinning blonde hair flapped in the wind, his cheeks and nose were already starting to turn red in the cool air.

There was something about the man's smile … it didn't quite reach his eyes. "A walk will do me good. 'Twas a bit pungent in there, was it no'?" he said with a slight chuckle.

While she agreed with him, she remained quiet and led the way. She had never been fond of the MacKinnon, but if he had any useful information, she might be willing to revisit her previous opinion of the man.

Fiona led him to the wide path that surrounded the keep. They were cast into shadows on the east side of the building. The air was even cooler here, out of the sun. The MacKinnon shivered slightly but made no move to quicken his step.

"So ye and the McDunnah are now allies?" he asked as they passed by a stone bench.

"Aye, we are," Fiona replied.

"He be a good man to have as an ally," Edgar said. "'Tis good to have more than one, however."

Fiona quirked a brow, but remained quiet. *Close yer mouth and open yer ears,* she heard her mother's words of wisdom echo in her mind.

"I never believed the McDunnah was responsible," Edgar said. "He's far too clever a man. And if Caelen wanted to attack ye, he'd let ye ken why. He'd want to take full credit and glory. Nay," he gave a shake of his head. "Nay, Caelen McDunnah is no' one to hide in the shadows like a coward."

Fiona could not argue with anything he had just said for that had been her own belief.

"Fiona, have ye any idea who might be responsible fer the raids?"

She had a few but she wasn't quite ready yet to share them with anyone outside her tight circle of brothers and advisors. "Nay, I fear I do no' ken who or why."

Edgar gave a knowing nod. "Would ye like me opinion on the matter?"

'Twas only morbid curiosity that moved her to answer aye.

"While I do no' ken who is behind the raids, mind ye, I believe they want us all to war with the McDunnah. Mayhap it be someone who seeks retribution fer some past deed done by the McDunnah, either real or imagined. Mayhap that someone is too small to take on the likes of the McDunnah on his own. So he does what he can to start a clan war."

Fiona wondered if Edgar didn't know more than he was telling. Mayhap he was giving her bits of information so that she could figure it out on her own. Or, he truly was just guessing.

"I had no' thought of that before, MacKinnon. I mean, I do believe someone might want us to be at war with the McDunnah, but I canna make a guess as to why. I suppose that be as good a reason as any." In the end the why was not nearly as important as the who.

"I could verra well be wrong. Then again, it could be someone from a larger clan or clans, who wants to start a war between all the clans, no matter the reason. The outcome would be the same."

Her curiosity was piqued. "What outcome?"

Edgar shrugged his shoulders as they rounded the corner and walked along the rear of the keep. "The outcome would be that we kill each other and they are left to pick through the spoils of war."

That was a terrifying prospect. If it was a larger clan or group of clans, they could easily start a war, sit back and wait until nothing was left of these smaller clans, such as her own. Greed was a tremendous motivator. Land could be far more valuable than gold. Was it possible that *that* was what this all boiled down to? Avarice?

"'Twould be better to let our smaller clans destroy one another, ye ken. They get all the gain without usin' any of their own vital resources."

What if he was correct? What if a larger clan, or worse yet *clans*, were at fault, just sitting back, stoking the flames of war? Would her clan be able to protect itself? What if the Farquar, McGregor, and McKenzie refused to believe such a possibility?

"And now that ye've declared the McDunnah yer ally — that is assumin' I'm right — the true culprits might begin raids on another clan and blame ye."

A chill ran down her spine with that thought. The mastermind behind the fake McDunnah attacks had almost succeeded. She thought back to the meeting. The McGregor did not seem convinced of Caelen's innocence and neither did the Farquar. How would she defend herself if she and her clan were suddenly made to look like raiders and murders?

"Again, I could be wrong, Fiona. It verra well could be somethin' as simple as someone hatin' the McDunnah enough they'd be willin' to do anythin' to bring him to his knees."

They walked along the rear of the keep, passing by chickens pecking at the ground and a small group of men huddled together under the eaves of the stable making bets on when the sun might shine again.

"I worry, Fiona, what will happen to ye and yers now that ye've publicly declared ye be allies with the McDunnahs."

Doubt began to creep in. She had meant her declaration as a warning to those in attendance that she had the force of the McDunnahs behind her. Her mind raced at all the new scenarios and possibilities.

"Fiona, the truth is it could be anyone doin' this fer any reason, whether it makes any good sense or no'. I ken ye said ye did no' want anyone's protection, but I beg ye to reconsider that. Ye might just need it more than ye realized."

Fiona came to an abrupt halt. Was this Edgar MacKinnon's way of terrifying her into a marriage?

Edgar smiled up at her. "I ken what yer thinkin' and nay, I be no' proposin' to ye again. I ken — and ye can correct me if I be wrong — that ye'll no' marry out of fear of either havin' to give up being chief or that yer clan will be absorbed into another."

Had Fiona been wrong about Edgar MacKinnon? He seemed to have a good grasp on exactly why she had turned down all those proposals. Mayhap he wasn't quite the weasel or weak-minded fool she had previously thought him to be.

"Ye be right, MacKinnon. I will no' give up bein' chief and I'll no' allow me clan to be lost to another." There were now new reasons why she'd never marry. Her heart thoroughly and completely belonged to Caelen McDunnah.

Edgar pursed his lips together and nodded again. "I canna say that I blame ye. Still, ye canna deny ye need protection. And I fear that mayhap the protection of the McDunnahs might no' be enough."

Doubt soon began to do serious battle to the certainty Fiona had previously possessed. Doubt about her clan's future, her people's safety and her ability to protect either.

Edgar MacKinnon walked beside her, seeming less and less the fool she had previously believed him to be. Mayhap he was wrong, mayhap he was right. Either way, there were new possibilities she would need to discuss with Collin and her advisors.

She began to miss her parents and Bridgett all the more. What she would not give for her parents' advice and Bridgett's shoulder. Had she not given in to temptation and lust two days ago, she would have gone straight to Caelen seeking his counsel on the matter.

She and Edgar were back where they had begun, walking across the front courtyard. When they neared the steps, Edgar gave a nod and waved his hand to ask if she would like to continue their walk. Fiona gave a nod of affirmation and a wan smile. Mayhap on their second trek around the keep, Edgar would have more answers than questions.

They walked quietly for a time. As the mist ebbed, a strong breeze pushed through, bringing with it the promise of rain. The men who had sought refuge under the eaves of the stables had disappeared, no doubt going back into the keep for more drink.

"Fiona," Edgar said, breaking through the quiet stillness. "I ken ye've no desire to marry me," he began. When he saw the *do no' dare ask again* flicker in Fiona's eyes, he laughed heartily.

His genuine laughter softened his features and made him seem less a greedy fool and more human.

"I was no' goin' to ask ye again, Fiona," Edgar said with a smile. "I learned me lesson the first time."

Fiona smiled back at him. "Good," she said.

"I ken ye will no' give up bein' chief nor will ye allow yer clan to be taken over by another."

Fiona tucked back errant strands of hair the breeze had loosened whilst she responded. "'Tis true. I'll do neither."

"I have another proposal fer ye," Edgar said as he clasped his hands behind his back. "One that will allow ye to remain chief, keep the McPhersons as McPhersons, but gain ye the numbers ye need in order to protect ye in case war does happen."

Thankful he wasn't proposing marriage again, Fiona smiled and bade him to continue.

"Before I go on, do I have yer word ye'll no' gut me?" Edgar asked playfully.

"Nay," Fiona answered. "I'll make no such promise. But I will promise to at least give ye a head start runnin'." Fiona was glad the mood between them had lightened. She was beginning to see Edgar in a different light. Mayhap he could someday be an ally and friend.

Edgar chuckled. "Thank ye." He fell silent for a moment before continuing. "I have a nephew, Fiona. He be a good man, a year younger than ye and if what the women of me clan say is true, he be a handsome one, too."

Fiona had a good suspicion as to where Edgar was heading with this conversation and she didn't like it.

"He be a good warrior as well and has a good head for strategy," Edgar tapped his temple with one finger.

It didn't matter to Fiona if the man resembled Adonis, had the stamina of a bull, or pockets full of gold. If she could not marry the man she loved, she'd marry no one. She remained quiet and allowed Edgar to continue listing all the fine attributes of his nephew.

"Like ye, he be widowed. I've left him to his grievin' these past years fer I knew how fond he was of the young woman. Margaret was her name."

At least 'twasn't Fiona, she mused.

"His wife died in childbed three years ago, but his daughter survived."

Fiona came to an abrupt halt and turned to study Edgar more closely. She saw no signs of deception in his eyes.

"Bhruic be a quiet man, with a good head on his shoulders, and a good heart. He works as hard on the battlefield as he does in our barley fields. He loves his wee one, little Aingealag. But he's come to realize he needs a wife and the babe needs a mother."

Aingealag, Fiona pondered the name. It meant angel. Until ten heartbeats ago, had anyone asked her if she would even consider marrying anyone other than Caelen McDunnah, she would have laughed herself silly. *A daughter,* she thought as her stomach tightened. A child she could call her own.

Edgar stared back at her, his expression holding nothing but kindness. "I do no' expect ye to answer me now, Fiona. I only ask that ye consider it. If ye accept, I give ye me word that Bhruic will treat ye kindly and he'll no' ever ask to become chief. And with him, I pledge one hundred fine soldiers."

As wonderful as the prospect of having a husband and a child might be, Fiona could not even consider it. She loved Caelen more than she had ever expected to love someone.

Two days ago, she'd left the shattered remnants of her heart at Caelen's keep. She could still see him standing there, his eyes filled with so much pain 'twas unbearable to remember it.

Now she stood before a man she had previously believed to be a greedy fool and he was offering her almost everything she ever wanted. *Almost.*

Five

After her conversation with Edgar MacKinnon, Fiona went to her room and remained there, more confused and miserable than she thought humanly possible. There were far too many losses for which to grieve over and even more things that needed consideration. Her head hurt, her bones ached and her heart felt beyond repair.

Usually, she would have bathed below stairs in the room off the kitchen but she had no desire to share her misery with anyone. She had a bath brought to her room where she soaked until her skin pruned, the water turned cold and she cried until she had no tears left.

With the little bits of her heart that remained, she yearned for Caelen. She missed everything about him. The way his eyes twinkled when he smiled or was being mischievous. The sound of his voice, his laughter, his smell. The way his calloused hands turned soft as silk against her skin. His breath upon her cheek, her neck, her lips. 'Twas a physical ache she felt to her marrow.

She wondered if he hurt as much as she and prayed that he didn't. 'Twas a torment she'd not wish on her worst enemy. While there might have been some satisfaction in knowing that he loved her as much as she loved him, she couldn't bear the thought of him being in this much agony.

She prayed that someday he would find it in his heart to forgive her. Mayhap if she knew he could and would, it might help to take some of the ache away.

Her justification for succumbing to her baser urges had made so much sense at the time. Believing she would never have another opportunity to be with Caelen in any physical sense, she thought she could join with him and take away nothing more than happy memories to keep her warm on cold nights. Now, she knew better.

It had been more than just a physical act to sate a desire. Aye, Caelen had sated her to the point of exhaustion. But it was so much more than that. He had *loved* her. 'Twas far more than simply two bodies writhing betwixt the sheets in blissful harmony. Caelen had shown her what it was like to be loved by a man, to be adored and cherished. He'd bared his heart to her and she'd torn it asunder.

The guilt was unbearable and something she doubted she'd ever be rid of.

Wrapped in a drying cloth, she sat on a stool in front of her hearth. Though the fire flickered and flared, it did nothing to warm the overwhelming cold that took up the space where her heart once beat.

'Twas not like her to be this melancholy, to feel so bereft and lost, but so much had happened in such a short amount of time. She had lost Bridgett, her dearest and most cherished friend to some murdering lunatic whose identity remained unknown. And she had lost the only chance at true love that had ever presented itself. A love as real as the sun or the moon or the mountain that stood tall and majestic behind her keep.

There was nothing to be done for it. She could no more be Caelen's wife than she could turn herself into a fairy.

Aye, she *could* have said yes, but in her heart she knew that eventually she would have grown to resent the decision. Accepting his proposal would have meant breaking her word to her father, to James and to his father. It would have meant letting her people down, disgracing herself before them by putting herself before them. The oath she'd taken the day she had become chief was the most important thing she'd ever done and it meant more to her than anything else. The oath, not the chiefdom itself, was more important than her own happiness or even Caelen.

Fiona realized she could not undo what she had done, yet it meant little at the moment. She had two choices — wallow in grief and self-pity or move forward. This was the path she'd chosen for herself, so move forward she must. Wiping her tears away with the backs of her hands, she took a deep breath and pushed herself to her feet. From the peg by the fire, she exchanged the drying cloth for her dark green robe.

From her trunk she grabbed a pair of dark leather trews, green tunic, clean undershirt, and woolens and placed them on the bed next to a simple brown dress.

Whilst she debated on what she should wear to the evening meal, her sister-in-law Isabelle knocked and announced herself. Fiona bade her to enter as she stood at the foot of the bed trying to decide what she should wear.

At any other time, she would have simply donned a simple dress. But she had five clan chiefs joining them for the evening meal. Should she dress as warrior or something more feminine?

"Good eve to ye, Fi," Isabelle said as she floated into the room. Isabelle was such a pretty young woman. How she put up with William's over-protective nature was beyond Fiona. Were she married to a man like her brother, she might very well be tempted to smash a heavy object against his head. Repeatedly. 'Twas likely that she would never have to worry over such a thing. 'Twas the only consolation she could make at the moment.

Isabelle's grace and elegance reminded Fiona so much of Bridgett. A pang of loss and regret stabbed at her heart.

"Isabelle," Fiona said as she stood staring at her choices of attire.

Isabelle giggled slightly as she came to stand next to Fiona. "Are ye tryin' to decide if ye should go as a warrior or a woman?"

Fiona smiled and gave a nod of her head. "It be so much easier fer men, aye? All they need do is don tunic and trews and plaid and they be done. I am both a warrior and a woman and I fear I've no' yet found the balance betwixt the two."

Isabelle placed a hand on her hip and looked at the leather and mail and plain brown dress Fiona had spread across the bed. "What are yer intentions with these men, Fi? Do ye wish them to ken that yer a warrior or an auld maid?"

Fiona raised a brow and stared at her sister-in-law for a moment. "What do ye mean?"

Isabelle picked up the hem of the plain brown dress. "Fi, this dress be so plain. Somethin' an auld woman would wear to clean house or pick berries. It be far too plain fer someone like ye."

Other than the brief time in her marriage when she tried to

seduce her less-than-enthusiastic husband, she hadn't really thought about how she dressed. It had been years since she'd worn anything other than serviceable dresses or her armor. There had been no one she needed to impress.

And until her few blissful hours with Caelen, she hadn't truly felt like a woman, at least not in the very feminine manner that Isabelle, Mairi and Bridgett had always seemed to possess so naturally. Her entire life, she had felt severely lacking in femininity.

Caelen had helped to change her opinion of herself, although she still firmly believed she was by no means as beautiful as he had declared her to be. Still, knowing he *believed* her beautiful was enough. She let out a sad sigh and shook her head. "In truth, I seek more comfort than message this night. My bones ache, Isabelle. I do no' fear anyone will think me less a warrior if I wear the simple brown dress."

"Fi, ye are a young, healthy, bonny woman. Why do ye hide it behind armor and mail or ugly, plain dresses?"

Fiona was taken aback by Isabelle's candid remark. "I may be somewhat young and healthy, but bonny?" she shook her head. "Even if I believed ye were tellin' the truth, there be no one here that I want to impress with me feminine wiles." She waggled her eyebrows playfully.

Isabelle pursed her lips together and said, "It matters no' if yer tryin' to impress anyone, it matters how *ye* feel. If ye would just listen to me, and wear a pretty dress, ye'll feel better."

Fiona shot her a look that said she seriously doubted it.

"I bet Mairi has somethin' ye could wear. She's no' nearly as tall as ye, but we could manage somethin', I'm certain."

Without waiting to hear all the reasons Fiona had for not wearing anything 'pretty' as her sister-in-law was suggesting, Isabelle left the room in a hurry.

"I be in no mood to be made a fool this night," Fiona murmured. She picked up the brown dress, folded it neatly and returned it to her trunk and returned to her bed. She was just about to pull on her under tunic when Isabelle and Mairi came into the room, all atwitter.

The eagerness and excitement that twinkled in their eyes sent an involuntary shiver down her spine. They looked far too happy, far too eager, and far too determined.

"I can dress meself, thank ye," Fiona said as she once again grabbed the dreary brown dress. "Ye can leave."

A knowing looking passed between Isabelle and Mairi. "Ye canna wear the brown dress. No' tonight, Fi. And we be no' sayin' ye need to dress like a harlot, just somethin' pretty," Mairi said sweetly.

"I have no need to feel 'pretty'," Fiona explained. "I only need to feel less tired and more comfortable."

"But, Fi," Isabelle said. "What would it hurt to let those fools below stairs ken that ye are no' just a chief? I myself would take great delight in makin' that point with them."

There was an unmistakable glimmer of anticipation and excitement in Isabelle's eyes. Fiona realized then that the young woman was a perfect match for William and might be the one person on God's earth that could keep her sometimes foolish brother in line.

Mayhap it would not hurt to wear something 'pretty' as her sisters-in-law were suggesting. Mayhap it might lift her spirits.

"Verra well, then," she told them. "But nothin' too revealin' or improper."

Isabelle and Mairi squealed with delight. "We promise," Mairi and Isabelle said in unison.

Somehow, Fiona didn't quite believe them.

With her shoulders back, and her head held high, Fiona floated down the stairs and into the gathering room, with Isabelle and Mairi thankfully right behind her. Feeling confident that her sisters-in-law were correct — a woman could be both warrior and feminine — she walked with all the grace and elegance she could muster. *Pretend ye are in battle* ... she repeated Isabelle's words over and over again in her mind as she made her way into the room. *Ye are quite graceful when yer fightin'.*

Men were gathered in groups that filled the room to near wall-bursting capacity. Boisterous laughter, heated arguments and general conversations slowly died away as all attention was turned toward Fiona.

She came face to face with a multitude of differing expressions. Everything from abject shock to intense curiosity, as if she were a selkie that had just emerged from a loch.

She had two choices. Start hurling daggers at them, or pretend 'twas just another day in her keep. Isabelle knew Fiona quite well and sensed she was reaching for a dagger. "Do no' do it," Isabelle whispered through a smile as she placed a hand on Fiona's arm.

"I do no' have enough daggers hidden to take them all down," Fiona whispered back. "Had ye let me—"

Isabelle cut her off mid-sentence, giving her hand a hard squeeze. "Had I let ye arm yerself from head to toe?" she asked as she pretended to look for someone in the crowd of wide-eyed, mouths-agaped men. "Remember who ye be and why yer here."

With that, she let go of Fiona's hand and gave her a gentle nudge forward. Were Isabelle not her sister-in-law, Fiona might have been tempted to give her latrine duty for the next year or two.

Swallowing back the rising humiliation, she stepped into the room, silently cursing Isabelle. *I shall never take Isabelle's advice on dresses ever again.* What with the low neckline and the way the emerald green dress lifted her bosom, the way it clung to her like a second skin, she might as well have been naked.

Silently, she made her way toward the dais, with Isabelle and Mairi right behind her. One man after another gave a nod or a polite bow as she walked by. Collin and William were already seated at the high table along with the five chiefs she had invited, and one man she did not recognize. She cursed inwardly with the only logical assumption available— the stranger was Bhruic MacKinnon. And someone had seated him in the honored place on her left.

Her ire rose rapidly. To have the man sitting in that particular spot — the spot reserved for honored guests or someone of exceptional importance on occasions such as these — might lead people to believe something that was not true. She would remedy that situation as soon as she got these men out of her keep.

Fiona made a mental note to find out just who amongst her family decided that was an appropriate place to put him. Punishment would be swift and severe.

The men at the table each stood, clearly surprised with how Fiona looked. Even the man she'd never met. He leaned sideways and whispered something into Edgar MacKinnon's ear. Edgar nodded and smiled before turning his attention back to Fiona. She could imagine the private conversation going something akin to *Uncle, ye did no' warn me she be so plain or so tall.*

Collin stepped away from the table and down the steps and extended his hand first to Fiona. As if she were too delicate a creature to make her own way up the stairs. She could have wrung his neck. They never stood on pretense like this. And what on earth was that stupid twinkle in Collin's eyes?

"Good eve, Fi," Collin said as he took her hand and led the way.

"Ye might want to sleep with one eye open this night, brother," she seethed in a harsh whisper.

He feigned confusion. "Whatever do ye mean?"

"Ye ken bloody well what I mean." She was unable to finish telling him exactly what she thought for they'd reached her chair. Collin pulled it out for her, something else that 'twas rarely done.

They wouldna be behavin' this way had I just worn me armor and mail, she grumbled inwardly as she sat down and looked out at the tables below and all the curious eyes staring back at her. She turned to look at her sisters-in-law who were just taking their seats. They smiled sweetly even though she cast them a dagger-filled glare of anger.

"Fiona," Edgar MacKinnon said. "I'd like ye to meet me nephew, Bhruic MacKinnon."

Knowing it would serve no useful purpose to cause a scene by hitting anyone over the head with her mug of ale, Fiona took a deep breath before turning in her seat to look up at the man.

The MacKinnon hadn't lied. Bhruic was quite handsome. Tall, taller mayhap than Caelen with blonde hair that hung past his shoulders. His blue eyes were as dark as indigo and his smile was brilliant. Handsome though he might be, he was not Caelen.

"Good eve," she said as nicely as she could manage under the circumstances. "'Tis a pleasure to meet ye."

Bhruic gave a slight bow and inclination of his handsome noggin. "I can assure ye, the pleasure is all mine."

Fiona ignored him and turned her attention back to the crowd. With her jaw clenched, she grabbed her tankard of ale and took a long drink. What she really needed was copious amounts of whisky and to be out of the dress that was too small, too tight, and far too revealing.

As she plotted how she'd get her revenge against Isabelle and

Mairi, servants began bringing out platters of food to the tables. When she spotted the fine fare — heaping platters of venison, beef and fish, bowl after bowl of vegetables and fruits — her eyes came close to bulging out of their sockets. What was her cook thinking, serving food fit for a king? Her ire simmered, just below the surface. There would be hell to pay for anyone party to such nonsense. They could ill afford to set out such delicious foods for their own clan, let alone so many guests.

Her appetite faded as she watched the spectacle play out before her. Finishing off her ale, she placed the tankard down and looked around the table for the whisky.

"Yer bein' rude to yer guests, Fi," Collin said as he leaned in.

Speaking in a harsh whisper, Fiona replied, "I'd no' be so rude had yer wife no' shoved me into this dress. I'd no' be so rude had anyone asked me what to serve fer the evenin' meal. And I'd no' be so bloody rude had someone asked me first who should be sittin' next to me!"

Collin looked puzzled. "I had nothin' to do with this. Mairi and Isabelle —"

"I knew it!" Fiona said exasperatedly as she spied the whisky in front of Collin. She grabbed it and filled her tankard halfway. "'Tis a good thing those women be married to me brothers or else I'd be sorely tempted to banish them fer their interference."

Collin chuckled and nodded in agreement. "I love me wife, I truly do," he said before turning quite thoughtful. "She means well, Fi. She wants to see ye happy, as we all do."

Fiona cast him a look that said she did not care what Mairi wanted for her. "How did she even ken about Bhruic or Edgar's proposal?" Fiona hadn't told anyone about Edgar MacKinnon's offer.

Collin quirked a curious brow. "What about Bhruic? What proposal?"

Fiona stared at him and sensed that he truly did not know about her earlier conversation with Edgar or his suggestion that she marry Bhruic. She looked away and took a drink of their fine whisky. "We will speak of it later."

Thankfully, Collin let the matter rest but Fiona knew he'd not forget or leave it rest for too long.

"I thank ye fer invitin' me to dine at yer table this night,"

Bhruic said.

Fiona began to count backwards from ten before turning to respond. He was quite handsome, if one liked blonde men with big, sparkling blue eyes. "Yer verra welcome," she said flatly.

A moment passed before Bhruic leaned in to speak in a low voice. "I have a feelin' ye were no' expectin' me."

How astute, she mused. And bluntly honest. Fiona could appreciate that in a person. "In truth?" she asked. "Nay, I was no'."

Bhruic smiled warmly. "I will apologize on behalf of me uncle's rudeness. He sometimes fergets he's only the chief of his clan, no' the king of Scotia."

She admired a man who was blunt and to the point and could not resist returning his smile. "I fear many a man suffers from the same affliction." She glanced down the table at her sisters-in-law. They looked positively gleeful as they pretended not to be watching her and Bhruic. "I also fear me sisters-in-law ferget they be no' the Queen."

Bhruic followed Fiona's gaze to the other end of the table. He laughed when Isabelle and Mairi found themselves caught. Their cheeks flamed red before they quickly turned away.

"Or the daughters of Cupid, aye?" Bhruic said with a chuckle.

Fiona laughed at his intuitive comment. "I suppose they mean well," Fiona said as she began to relax.

"I wish I could say the same fer me uncle," Bhruic said. "I fear he has ulterior motives."

Fiona's brow raised sharply. "Such as?"

Bhruic laughed and took another drink of ale. "Nothin' ugly, I can assure ye. I fear he wishes to be nothin' more than a hero of sorts."

Edgar MacKinnon, a hero? 'Twas as confusing a notion as any.

Bhruic explained himself further. "He kens yer plight, me lady, what with the raids and senseless murder of one of yer women—"

"Ye may call me Fiona," she interjected. "And her name was Bridgett." Her smile faded. Collin nudged her with one elbow, offering her the platter of venison. Fiona declined with a raised hand.

"Verra well," Bhruic replied as he took the platter Collin offered. "As I was sayin', me uncle does have ulterior motives, ye see." He took two slices of venison and dropped them onto his trencher before handing it off to his uncle.

"He wants to be a hero?" Fiona asked quietly.

"Aye," Bhruic answered as he cut the venison into smaller bites. "He thinks that if he can stop the raids or more senseless murders, he'll be looked upon as a hero."

Fiona swallowed a laugh behind a drink of warm whisky. Aye, if anyone could stop the raids and root out who was behind them, then aye, they'd be a hero in her eyes. She could not help but wonder, however, if heroic deeds were Edgar's only motivation.

"Do ye always serve such fine fare as this?" Bhruic asked as he savored the tender venison.

"Nay, we do no'," she said. "I fear me family wanted to make a good impression on our guests." *Even if it meant an empty larder when the night was done.*

"I fear I'd much prefer a simpler meal, one without all the pageantry and pretense," Bhruic said. "Although, I must admit, yer cook has done quite well. Ye should try the venison," he said as he cut a piece from what little was left on his trencher and placed it onto hers.

The gesture of sharing his food with her was far too intimate for her liking. Aye, it might have been born out of simple kindness and the fact that he did not know her well. She could feel Isabelle and Mairi staring at her, watching her every move. Knowing the two women as she did, if she were to eat the bit of offered meat they'd take it as a proposal of marriage and would immediately set out making plans for a wedding. "Thank ye, but I do no' care fer venison." While 'twasn't necessarily her favorite choice in meat, she would not have turned it down under different circumstances. Being raised as she had, any meat was a welcome addition to any meal. This was different. 'Twas merely her way of letting him know she was not some delicate flower who needed to be fed or have her meat cut.

Without saying a word, Bhruic took the meat back and plopped it into his own mouth. "Good," he said as he chewed. "I didna want to share it with ye anyway."

Then he winked at her, signifying he was only being playful.

Fiona wasn't quite sure what to make of this man. He was being blunt, open, and mayhap a bit bold in treating her as if they had been friends since they were weans. Either 'twas simply his nature to be so open with someone he did not know or he was trying to impress her. She'd wait to pass judgment.

Over the course of the meal, Fiona's appetite began to return. Bhruic seemed to be a pleasant enough fellow. While most of his attention was focused on her, he did manage to have a conversation with Collin about sheep. She only half-listened as her mind tried to work out if anyone in the room might be the bastard responsible for Bridgett's murder.

Was there one among the dozens gathered here dumb enough or arrogant enough to kill Bridgett only to turn around and sit at Fiona's table? Kill then partake of the festivities?

The only one with the appropriate amount of arrogance was Aric MacElroy. But Fiona had serious doubts that he'd have the intestinal fortitude necessary to kill anyone. Nay, he'd not want to mess up his fine silk tunic or his carefully manicured hands. He might, however, be inclined to have one of his own men do such a horrendous deed. Mayhap he had hired mercenaries? Nay, he'd not part with his precious coin. Still, she would not put the man past doing such a thing.

"What be yer opinion on the matter, Fiona?" 'Twas Collin who asked the question, drawing her out of her meandering thoughts.

"I be afraid I was no' listenin'," she told him.

Before Collin could comment, Bhruic touched her forearm and said, "I was just askin' why a bonny woman such as ye was no' already married."

Fiona heard Collin and Mairi take a collective breath and hold it.

Bhruic smiled, unaware of her extreme dislike of untrue compliments. She was reaching for the *sgian dubh* hidden under the long sleeve of her dress when Collin stopped her with a firm hand on hers.

It took a few moments of uneasy silence before Bhruic realized something was the matter. His smile changed to a look of perplexity. "What?" he finally asked.

Fiona removed her hand from Collin's with a yank and turned to look at Bhruic. Before she could utter a word, Mairi spoke up. "Fergive her Bhruic, but me sister-in-law does no' like compliments."

Fiona stared at Mairi as if she'd lost her mind. 'Twas a tremendous understatement on her part.

Bhruic looked even more confused. "I do no' understand?" He looked Fiona directly in the eye. "I meant no offense, me lady, only to compliment ye."

Fiona began counting to one hundred.

"Fi, he was only bein' kind," Collin whispered, his voice warning her to keep her temper.

"By lyin'?" Fiona asked harshly.

Bhruic's shoulders drew back as he scowled at her insult. "I was no' lyin', my lady. I do find ye quite bonny and why ye'd take that as an insult is beyond me comprehension."

"I be no' some naive young lass, Bhruic, who needs her feminine ego caressed. Ye can take yer false compliments and—"

Before she could tell him exactly where he could put his false compliments, Mairi jumped to her feet and came to pull Fiona away from the table. "Fiona," she said, sounding quite frustrated. "Ye need to come with me fer a moment."

Fiona looked up at Mairi who looked quite determined to get her away from the table. Isabelle was soon standing next to her. Each of them pleaded silently for Fiona to follow.

"Verra well," she said as she pushed away from the table and stood. Before leaving, she looked first to Bhruic then to Collin. Collin looked as though he wanted to say something but thought better of it. "Explain the way of things to him," she told her oldest brother as she gestured at Bhruic. "And make sure he understands."

William was on his feet and whispering something to his wife. Fiona thought his countenance odd for his face held a look of fear. What on earth was the matter with him? They looked to be in a heated discussion but over what, she didn't rightly know. She ignored them as she followed Mairi out of the gathering room and up the stairs.

Mairi led the way down the hall and into Fiona's private chambers. There was no doubt that she was upset, but over what, Fiona could not begin to guess.

"It be time ye put away yer ridiculous belief that yer no' bonny," Mairi said as she stood next to the hearth. Her jaw was set, her voice firm, and the fiery resolve in her eyes unmistakable.

"Mairi—" she tried to speak, but Mairi would have none of it.

"Hear me out, please." 'Twas more of a demand she made than a request. "I be quite serious about this, Fiona. 'Tis time ye knew the truth—"

Before she could finish, Isabelle came rushing into the room with William in fast pursuit. Isabelle slammed the door shut, pulled down the bar before turning around, out of breath.

"Did ye tell her yet?" Isabelle asked while William pounded on the door, demanding entry.

"I was just about to," Mairi answered.

"Isabelle!" William bellowed. "Open this door this instant."

"Nay!" Isabelle shouted back. "Be gone with ye!"

Mairi glanced at the door and cringed as William continued to shout and pound his fists against the heavy wooden door. Isabelle rolled her eyes, keeping her back pressed tightly against the door, as if her wee frame could keep her husband from knocking the door down. "Ye best hurry, Mairi!" Isabelle said. "I do no' ken how long I can hold him at bay!"

"I swear, Isabelle, when I get me hands on ye, ye'll no' be able to sit fer a week!" William bellowed from the other side.

Isabelle rolled her eyes and scoffed at his threat and yelled at him through the door. "Bah! Ye'll do no such thing, William McCray! Yer sister would have yer head if ye so much as think of layin' an angry finger to me!" She turned back to Mairi. "Ye best hurry!"

Fiona was quite certain the three of them had lost their minds. "Yer all daft," she told them.

"Fiona," Mairi said as she rushed across the room and took Fiona's hands in hers. "I need ye to listen, but first I need ye to promise ye'll no' take anyone's life."

"Not bloody likely," Fiona countered. William was now pounding against the door with such force that it jostled Isabelle. "Let the eejit in, Isabelle. Now."

"But he doesna want us to tell ye!" Isabelle argued.

"Now." Fiona had reached the end of her patience.

"But—" Isabelle continued to protest. Once she realized Fiona was not going to listen, her shoulders sagged as she let loose a sorrowful sigh. Slowly she unbarred the door and opened it.

William, his face red with anger, came rushing into the room. "No matter what they told ye, 'tis a lie!'"

Aye, they'd all lost their minds, Fiona was quiet certain of it. "Yer all bein' quite ridiculous," she said before turning to look at Mairi. "Now, what is it that ye want to tell me that me brother does no' want me to hear?"

William stepped forward, "They've nothin' to tell ye—"

Mairi cut him off. "William, she needs to ken and she needs to ken now. 'Tis absurd what ye and yer family have done to her all these years! She verra well could have killed that man below stairs, and fer what? A foolish lie!"

Fiona hid her bewilderment and curiosity behind a fierce scowl. "I have had enough. William, if ye utter another word, I shall cut out yer tongue," she looked directly at her brother. He rolled his eyes in defeat and sat down on the edge of Fiona's bed.

Fiona turned back to Mairi and Isabelle. With a nod of her head, she bade them to continue.

Mairi took a deep breath and began to wring her fingers together nervously. "I ken ye think yer no' bonny, Fiona, but that be no' true."

Good Lord, Fiona thought to herself.

"But ye see, that be no' necessarily true," Isabelle added, looking just as nervous as Mairi.

"Aye, it be no' true at all." Mairi agreed.

Her patience gone, the subject of their discussion beyond humiliating, Fiona threw her hands in the air. "All of ye are daft! I've no desire to discuss whether or no' I be bonny. 'Tis absolutely of no import to me."

Mairi and Isabelle cast wary glances at one another. Mairi took a step toward Fiona. "But ye need to ken the truth of it, Fiona, if only so ye do no' feel moved to killin' a man over a simple compliment."

Fiona let out an exasperated sigh. "Fine. I be as bonny as the day be long. Are ye happy?"

From behind her, William groaned his frustration. "Fiona," he said as he stood up and walked toward her. "What Isabelle and Mairi are tryin' to tell ye is that ye *are* quite bonny."

'Twas the first time in her whole life that her brother ever said such a thing. There was no way to hide her stunned surprise.

"Ye see, when ye were born, ye were so verra bonny. Everyone remarked about it. Anyone who came to see ye said the same thing *What a beautiful babe, she'll never want fer anythin'*."

She could not have been more stunned had he just told her she was the bastard child of Robert the Bruce. Knitting her brows together, she said, "Nay, I ken the truth, William. I was *no'* a bonny babe. Everyone said so."

William shook his head in disagreement. "Nay, our *mum* said so."

Fiona stood there, stunned into temporary silence. A long moment passed between them as Fiona tried to make sense of what he was saying. She was unsuccessful. "I fear I do no' understand. Why on earth would mum say such a thing? For what end?"

William raked a hand through his dark hair and let out a breath of frustration. His blue eyes held a sadness that she'd never witnessed before. "Mayhap we should sit," he said as he guided her toward the hearth. After arranging the two chairs to face one another, he sat his sister down.

"Before I begin, ye must ken that mum meant well. She had good reasons fer doin' what she did."

Fiona sat with her shoulders back, trying to mentally prepare herself for whatever her brother was about to tell her.

"Our mum had a sister, Ariana was her name," William began.

Fiona tried to pull some memory from her past where the name Ariana was mentioned. Her mother had come from Clan Maclan and rarely spoke of her family. Fiona had always assumed her mother's lack of speaking about her family meant she'd not had the best of upbringings and never pushed her mother to tell more.

"Mum was the youngest of three daughters, ye see. Margaret was the oldest, then Ariana, then our mum. Accordin' to mum, Ariana was spoiled beyond belief by their parents, our grandparents. Ariana was a beautiful child who grew into an even more beautiful young woman. Her entire life, anyone could speak of was Ariana's beauty. She had thick dark hair and mesmerizin' emerald green eyes."

Their mum had been breathtakingly beautiful. It was difficult for Fiona to imagine a beauty to rival hers.

"Now, mum and Margaret were verra close to one another. They tried to be close to Ariana, but accordin' to our mum, Ariana had a black heart that her parents chose to ignore and it only grew blacker as she grew. I be no' sayin' that mum and Margaret were abused or neglected fer they were no'. Their parents were good people, but their da, well, there was just somethin' about Ariana. When Margaret was seventeen, she fell verra much in love with Charles Maclan, the second born son of their chief. Charles loved Margaret too, loved her verra much. One night, he came to see mum's da and ask fer Margaret's hand. Ariana was verra jealous that Margaret might marry the son of their chief. Ye see, Charles older brother Rolph was already married. Ariana's only hope at marryin' into the chief's family was through Charles. She wanted the status more than the man. So she made an accusation that Charles had seduced her and she carried his babe."

The story was making Fiona's head swim. Why had her mother never shared any of this with her, her only daughter?

"Of course Margaret didna believe Ariana, but their da did. He refused to allow Margaret to marry the man who supposedly took advantage of his innocent, beautiful Ariana. He went straight to their chief that verra night and insisted Charles marry Ariana. Och, she put on such a gallant show, according to our mum, all teary-eyed, contrite and ashamed. The chief chose to believe his son over Ariana. Their da flew into a rage that the chief would call his Ariana a liar. Before anyone could react, their da drew his sword and plunged it into their chief's belly. A moment later, Charles killed mum's da, our grandda."

William nodded when Fiona gasped and covered her mouth with her fingers. "Aye, 'twas a horrible event."

"Good, lord, what happened next?" Fiona managed to ask.

"Ariana felt no guilt over what she'd caused. None whatsoever. Margaret and mum, however, were broken-hearted, beyond consolation. Their poor mum died just a few weeks later, some say from a broken heart. But Ariana? Not one tear did the woman shed over the loss of her parents, over the loss of their chief, or for any of the misery she caused. Not long after, she packed up and moved to Inverness where she managed to marry into nobility. Margaret did marry Charles, months later, and mum soon married our da. Neither Margaret nor mum truly ever got over the loss of their parents and they never saw Ariana, again."

Fiona sat in dumbfounded silence. 'Twas a disturbing tale, to be certain. Suddenly, she was quite glad she hadn't been blessed with a sister. But what had any of that to do with her? "'Tis a sad tale ye tell me, William, but I fear I do no' understand why ye were afraid to tell me."

William looked somewhat sheepish before he went on to explain. "Ye see, Fiona, when mum heard all the compliments people were givin' when ye were born, she grew fearful of how 'twould affect ye as ye grew aulder. Her biggest fear was that ye might turn out like Ariana. She could no' bear the thought. So she made us all swear we'd never compliment ye on how bonny ye were. After she told us the why of it, we felt so sorry for her that we agreed. Mum wanted ye to be known fer a kind heart or fer bein' intelligent or graceful or anythin' else but how bonny ye were."

"That be the most ridiculous thing I have ever heard in me life," Fiona told him. "Ye canna be serious?"

"I be afraid that I am. So we never again remarked at how pretty ye might be. We did our best to encourage ye in other ways, such as with yer knives, yer quick wit and yer kind heart."

There was no way to be angry with her mother. Her brothers however, were an entirely different matter. Not because she was in any way vain or uncomfortable in her own skin, but because they had withheld this information from her her whole life. They could have, at one point or another, pulled her aside and told her the truth.

"Ye could have told me this before, William," she said as she shot to her feet and began pacing. "Mayhap when I was four and ten and cryin' me eyes out because when I tried to kiss Donnel McFarland, he turned white as a sheet and ran away from home for three days, leavin me to think 'twas because I was so bloody hideous!" She spun around and glared at him. "Or a year later, when I finally got up the nerve to ask Peter McPherson to dance at the Hogmanay feast. The poor lad turned green before me eyes and ran out of the keep like banshees were chasin' after him!"

William remained guiltily silent, looking at the hearth, the floor at his feet, the ceiling, anywhere but at Fiona. "There be more yer no' tellin' me, William. Out with it."

He shrugged his shoulders and pretended not to know what she meant.

Isabelle and Mairi finally stepped forward to chastise her brother. "Tell her the rest, William," Isabelle said, her arms crossed over her chest and a scowl fierce enough to scare the devil.

He remained quiet.

"Ye tell her or I will," Isabelle threatened.

"I fear I do no' ken what ye want me to say. I've told her everythin'."

Isabelle pursed her lips together before turning to look at Fiona. "The lads didna run because they thought ye hideous or homely or even plain. They ran and hid because yer brothers threatened *all* of them with death if they so much as glanced yer way."

'Twas all too ridiculous for words. A low laugh began in her belly and continued to grow until Fiona was laughing to the point of hysteria. This had to be some sort of jest. A lie. She knew, deep down, that she was not as pretty as Mairi or Isabelle or as Bridgett had been. She knew it, unequivocally, undeniably. Aye, Caelen thought she was quite bonny, but everyone knew he was a bit tetched. She had taken everything he had told her with a grain of salt, believing 'twas her personality or her keen wit or her fine skills as a warrior that had attracted him to her.

Her laughter filled the room and she was unable to control it. Out of breath, she plopped down in the chair, holding her sides, as her family continued to stare at her with increasing concern.

"Yer all daft! Every bloody last one of ye!" Fiona blurted out before bursting into another fit of hysterical laughter.

"Fiona," Mairi asked, her voice filled with unease. "What be so funny?"

Fiona shook her head. "I dunnae!" she said between bouts of laughter. "'Tis all too ludicrous!"

Three pairs of baffled eyes stared at her.

"I fear that if I do no' laugh, I'll end up in tears," Fiona admitted as her laughing began to subside. "'Tis much to take in, ye ken. To think that me whole life I could have had men eatin' out of the palm of me hand!"

Unfortunately, neither her brother nor her sisters-in-law saw the humor in the situation.

Truthfully, she wasn't certain how she felt about it. Should she be angry and upset? Should she go spit in the wind at what her mother had done to her? Leaving her to believe all these many years that she wasn't quite pretty enough or bonny enough to turn a man's head?

What did it matter? Would she see herself differently now? Did it truly change anything? Nay, she supposed, it did not. She was still the chief of her clan, still the same Fiona McPherson that she'd always been. The only difference would be that if someone were to by some chance give her a compliment in the future, she wouldn't be tempted to take out her dirk and stab him in the eye.

Six

Caelen and his men arrived at the MacDougall keep long after the midnight hour. Caelen had pushed his men and their horses to their limits on their journey north. By the time they reached MacDougall lands, they were covered with filth, sweat and grime and on the brink of exhaustion. The moon hung high and brilliant overhead as a heavy breeze rattled against man and earth alike.

Caelen did not care. There was too much at stake to dally along the way. If there was anyone on God's earth who could help him, 'twas Angus McKenna, chief of Clan MacDougall.

Caelen and his men climbed down from their mounts as they waited outside the gates of Castle Gregor. 'Twas one of the largest castles outside of Stirling or Edinburgh. Three stories high with four tall square towers, the massive structure was simple in its majesty. It did not boast loudly of opulence or richness, though the MacDougalls were powerful enough and rich enough to make such claims if they chose. Nay, Castle Gregor bespoke power, but instead of shouting its message, it whispered. 'Twas a quiet reflection of the men and women within.

The wait was not long and soon Caelen and his men were allowed inside the walls. At this late hour, most people were asleep save for the night watchmen. One of the MacDougall men approached as the McDunnahs made their way across the large open courtyard.

"Good eve, to ye. The McKenna awaits ye indoors," the slender young man told Caelen. "I can see to yer men and to yer horses if ye'd like."

Caelen was glad for the offer. "Thank ye, kindly. I ken me men are tired and hungry after our journey."

Caelen found Kenneth in the middle of the small crowd. "I would like ye to go with me to talk to Angus."

"Verra well," Kenneth said as he and Caelen handed their horses off to Obert. "No rest fer the wicked, aye?"

Caelen chuckled slightly as they headed toward the MacDougall keep. "Mayhap that be why neither of us get much sleep."

Though the breeze was not quite as strong inside the walls as out, 'twas still strong enough. Caelen's plaid flapped against his chest and 'twas then he caught a whiff of his foul-smelling self. There was no time to waste by jumping in the loch. Angus would have to take them as they were.

Caelen and Kenneth had been escorted into the empty, dark grand gathering room. Warming themselves by the fire, they watched as Angus made his way down the staircase. Angus McKenna, though more than fifty summers auld, was still as tall and powerful as he'd been in his youth. Aye, there may have been a few wrinkles around his bright green eyes, and his blonde hair may have been more white but he was still an imposing a figure as ever there was. Though 'twas the middle of the night, Angus was dressed in dark trews and fine blue tunic. The man looked to be both curious and glad to see his friend.

"Caelen," Angus said as he made his way to the hearth. "What the bloody hell are ye doin' here at this ungodly hour?" He smiled as he extended his arm.

Caelen wrapped his hand around Angus' massive forearm and drew him in, giving him a hearty slap on the back. "I missed yer bonny face, ye auld curmudgeon."

Angus laughed as he pounded Caelen's back. "'It has been too long since last we've seen ye here," he said before recognizing Kenneth. "And even longer fer ye, Kenneth."

"At least five years I believe," Kenneth said as he shook Angus' offered arm.

"Six," Angus corrected him as he took a step back and studied Caelen and Kenneth closely for a moment. "'Tis no' a social visit that brings ye here."

Caelen cleared his throat before answering. "Nay, 'tis no'."

Angus gave him a knowing nod. "Do we need the war room, or me private study?"

"Fer now, I think yer private study will suffice," Caelen answered.

Angus let out a relieved sigh. "Good, fer I fear I be gettin' far too auld fer battle," he said with a chuckle as he began to lead the men up the stairs. Angus' private study was on the second floor of the massive keep.

"Ye?" Caelen chuckled. "Ye'll still be fightin' the day the good Lord calls ye from His earth."

Angus laughed, his booming voice echoing off the stone walls. "I hope to hell no'! When me time comes, I want it to be whilst I'm in the safe and lovin' confines of me wife's arms."

When they had entered Angus' private study, the sky was as black as pitch. By the time Caelen finished telling Angus all that had transpired over the past few weeks, dawn was just beginning to break. The early morning sky was a beautiful blend of indigo, gray, and pink.

They sat opposite one another in front of the hearth, with Angus asking an occasional question. Kenneth sat beside Caelen, offering tidbits of information. Caelen did most of the talking.

"So there ye have it," Caelen said as he held his empty palms upward, "and why I be here today."

Angus pursed his lips and thought hard for a long moment. "'Tis unusual for the Highlands to be so quiet on a matter," Angus remarked. "A man in Inverness can pass gas while breakin' his fast and his cousin in Mull will ken of it by the noonin' meal."

Caelen chuckled at his friend's assessment. Gossip flowed as easily as wind and water. "I canna even find the smallest hint as to who may be behind these attacks. I canna believe this all came about over supposed magic water."

"I would no' be so quick to dismiss it, Caelen. Men have been moved to do far worse fer far less," Angus said.

Caelen knew Angus was right. Nothing about this entire ordeal made any sense. "Even if they are motivated out of some misguided notion that the water on Fiona's lands is magic, that still does no' explain why they've involved *me*. Why make me look guilty? What possible gain could come of that?"

Angus' brows drew into a knot as he thought on it. "Be it possible the two are no' related? That those chiefs are proposin' fer magic water, but whoever is raidin' and blamin' ye is a separate matter altogether?"

"We've given that much thought," Kenneth added. "But we believe it be far too coincidental."

"Aye," Angus said thoughtfully. "None of us believes in coincidence."

Caelen smiled and stretched his long legs out. "Nay, we do no' believe in coincidence."

"What would ye like from me, Caelen? What can I do to help? Are ye here to invoke the Bond of the Seven?"

Caelen sat forward in his chair, resting his elbows on his knees. "I believe it be too early yet, to do that." The Bond of the Seven Clans had been forged between the MacDougalls, McDunnahs, McKees, Lindsays, Randolphs, Carruthers and Grahams ages ago. 'Twas a promise made that should one clan need the others, all they need do is invoke the bond and the others would be there to offer whatever assistance they could. "Fer now, I would like yer help, and Nial's, in findin' out who be determined to see me either ruined or dead."

"I received word from Nial earlier this night. He and Bree shall be arrivin' in three days," Angus said.

"Three days?" Caelen asked, disheartened over the news.

"Aye, he had some business to settle before he could leave. What that business was, I do no' ken. But he'll be here."

Knowing there was nothing to be done over it, Caelen let out a long breath. "Could ye send out yer own spies? Mayhap they will be successful where mine were no'."

Angus gave a slight nod and said, "Aye, I shall dispatch them this morn."

Caelen yawned, the exhaustion beginning to settle into his bones. He could not remember the last time he slept well or for more than a few hours at a time. If he wasn't running around the countryside, his dreams were plagued with images of Fiona.

"It has been a verra long night," Angus said as he pushed himself to stand. "Ye can have Duncan's auld room while yer here. I recommend ye get as much sleep as ye can, fer it might be some time before ye have it again."

Caelen smiled wryly at the mention of his old friend's name. "How be Duncan? And Aishlinn?"

Angus smiled proudly and said, "They be well. They have six children now. Four boys and two daughters."

A pang of envy stabbed at his chest. Forcing a smile he stood and said, "That be a lot of children."

Angus nodded in agreement. "Aye, 'tis. Mayhap someday ye'll find the right woman to settle down with and have a dozen of yer own."

A sharp pain of regret stabbed at his heart. He was not quite ready yet to divulge to Angus his true feelings for Fiona McPherson. "Mayhap, someday," he said with a false smile. *If God is willing and allows me to find a way.*

Seven

Fiona had just finished explaining Edgar MacKinnon's proposal to William and Collin and their wives. They sat now, in silence, around the table in Fiona's study. For a long time, none of them said a word.

"I've spent only a small amount of time with Bhruic these past two days," Collin said as he glanced first at his wife, then to Fiona. "He be a good man. I like him."

Mairi placed a hand on Collin's arm. "But Fiona does no' love him, Collin."

Collin patted Mairi's hand. "I ken that. But unfortunately, she be no' in a position to take love into consideration."

Mairi began to protest at her husband's insensitivity. He stopped her with a wave of his hand. "Mairi, ye ken as well as I that what I say be true. Fiona is chief. Marriage for her — or any chief for that matter — is no' always a matter of the heart, but a matter of what is best fer the clan."

"True or no', 'tis no' fair that she has to be forced into a marriage without consideration of her heart," Mairi argued.

"Think of what it would mean fer the clan," William interjected. "'Twould mean gainin' good fightin' men that we need."

Isabelle looked at her husband with mouth agape, utterly stunned that he would agree to such a union. "William! Ye of all people? Ye've always been Fiona's champion and now ye throw away all regard fer her feelin's just to gain more men?"

"I do no' throw away all me regard, Isabelle. If I did no' like

Bhruic, I'd be against this just as much as ye." He glanced at Fiona then and said, "Besides, she would be gainin' a daughter."

Of all the people in the room, William knew how desperately Fiona wanted a child of her own. Fiona gave him a modest smile but remained quiet.

Isabelle threw her hands up in frustration. "I be surprised at the both of ye," she said. "Ye were against all the other proposals 'til this one. Ye make no sense!"

"Aye," Mairi agreed. "Fiona turned down every proposal to date and ye supported her decision. Even after the raids began, ye said no to Fiona marryin' anyone. I do no' understand either of ye."

"Aye," Collin said. "We were against Fiona marryin' another *chief.* That would have meant us losin' our name, our identity, our history. This be different."

"How?" Mairi asked, dismayed by her husband's turn in opinion.

"It be different because with this marriage, Fiona remains chief, Clan McPherson remains Clan McPherson, we get one hundred strong fightin' men. Fiona no' only gets a child she can call her own, but a good husband who likes her and finds her quite bonny," Collin explained.

Fiona had heard enough. "Ye all make valid arguments fer and against this union," she said as she drew circles on the table with her index finger. "But in the end, the decision is still mine to make. I ken we need more men. I ken we need strong allies, and we would have that with the MacKinnon."

While she may have known those things to be true, it did not mean she enjoyed the thought of having to make this decision.

"I will no' make the decision lightly, ye have me word," she told them as she pushed herself away from the table. "The hour is late so I shall now bid ye all good night." With a nod of her head, she quit the room and went to her bedchamber.

Fiona's mind would not settle, would not allow her the sleep she desperately needed. Each time she closed her eyes she would see Caelen's face, filled with pain, pain she had caused him.

An ache had settled deep in her heart. An ache so profound and intense that she did not think she would ever be rid of it. Alone in her room, she sat on the wide windowsill, wrapped in a blanket, chilled to the bone. She stared out across the rocky land into the indigo sky, sprinkled with stars and a crescent moon. And she wept quietly, praying and wishing for things she could not have.

The wound of having to leave Caelen, of having to turn away the chance at being his wife, was still so fresh and raw. Fiona wondered if 'twould ever heal or if 'twould simply continue to fester until she was nothing but a shell of the woman she had once been.

It had only been less than a sennight since last she'd seen him, but much had happened since she'd left the man she loved on the steps of his keep. When she'd left him there, she thought it had been the single most difficult decision of her life. Now? Now she was forced to make another that would, she knew, be even more difficult. Marry a man she did not love and knew she never would in order to secure the future and safety of her clan. Or, turn down the offer, and leave her clan vulnerable to more attacks, more raids, and the potential loss of more lives.

Oh, how she wished Bridgett were here to help her, to offer solid advice, a word of comfort. Bridgett would have understood how difficult this decision was and would have done her best to help Fiona through it, no matter which path she took.

How could she say yes and marry a man, who, though she liked him well enough, she could not imagine ever loving, at least not in the same way she loved Caelen? How could she willingly go to the altar and make a promise to love and honor Bhruic? 'Twould not be fair to either of them or to Caelen.

How could she take another man into her bed and share her body with him? The thought brought forth more tears. In her heart, she knew that if she did say yes and marry Bhruic, every time he touched her she would think of Caelen. It would be Caelen's lips she wanted pressed passionately against her own. And Caelen's hands she would want and imagine gently caressing her skin, not Bhruic's. And she was sure it would be Caelen's voice she would hear whispering sweet words in her ears, his hot breath upon her skin, not Bhruic's.

The marriage would be nothing but a lie from the beginning.

'Twould change her, 'twould make her a liar and she'd no longer be the woman she once was. The guilt would be unbearable.

Fiona woke to the morning light feeling just as confused and contrary as when she had fallen asleep. No new answers had miraculously arrived whilst she slept. No fail-proof plan had come to mind for a way out of the mess she found herself in. She hadn't fallen out of love with Caelen nor had she received a divine message from God telling her who had killed her best friend. In short, nothing had changed.

She slid from her bed, splashed cold water on her face, washed her teeth and dressed. The clan chiefs were set to leave after breaking their fast. Whilst she'd have preferred to remain in her room, there was too much to do. First on her list was telling Edgar MacKinnon thank ye, but no thank ye. She couldn't marry Bhruic.

She made her way down the stairs and into the gathering room. It looked to be every bit as full as the night before. Secretly, she had hoped that they'd all be gone by the time she made her way below stairs.

Cursing under her breath the lot life had dealt her, she made her way to the dais where Collin and Mairi were already seated. Mairi was feeding wee Symon little bits of bread and eggs. He was such a sweet babe, all cheeks and thick eyelashes and drool. Happily chomping away at bits of bread, not all of it making its way into his belly. God in heaven, what she would not do to have a babe of her own.

As she made her way to the front of the gathering room, she caught sight of Edgar MacKinnon on the opposite side of the room. Fiona made her way through the crowded space to speak with him. "Good morn, Edgar," Fiona said, forcing a smile.

"Ah! Good morn to ye as well, Fiona," he said cheerfully.

'Twas far too crowded at the moment to have the conversation she needed to. "After ye break yer fast, could ye please join me in me study?"

Edgar smiled and said, "Of course. Shall I bring Bhruic?"

"Nay, that will no' be necessary."

For a fleeting moment, his smile disappeared. "Verra well," he said with a curt nod. "After we break our fast."

Fiona thanked him and went to sit with her family. "Good morn, Collin, Mairi," she said as she made her way up the steps. As she passed behind them, she paused to kiss the top of Symon's head. "And good morn to ye, ye wee beastie," she said playfully.

When he looked up to smile at her, she noticed a bump on his forehead "What be this? Were ye wounded in battle, wee one?"

Mairi rolled her eyes and shook her head. "Nay, he's taken to pullin' himself up to things," she explained. "But he does no' realize not everythin' be sturdy. He tried pullin' himself up to the stool I sit upon fer sewin'. It flipped over, and knocked him right in his wee head." Mairi placed a motherly kiss on his little bump. "I be surprised ye didna hear him screamin'! 'Twas loud enough to wake the dead."

Fiona laughed and took her seat. "I fear the lack of sleep finally caught up with me last night. Hordes of Huns could have attacked and I'd have slept through it."

Collin finished shoveling eggs into his mouth and downed the rest of his cider before taking Symon into his own lap. "What say we let yer beautiful mum eat, Symon?"

Symon cooed and laughed as Collin bounced him on his knee. "Ye'll be walkin' before long, aye?" he asked Symon. "That will be when all the fun starts."

Fiona was enjoying Symon's giggles and coos, when something out of the corner of her eye caught her attention. Why it drew her attention, she could not rightly say. Nonetheless, she looked up to see Bhruic standing in the entry way. He was not alone.

Alyse McPherson was with him.

Alyse was a quiet woman, just a year or two younger than Fiona. And like Fiona and Bhruic, she was widowed. Alyse had come from the MacKinnon clan six years ago when she married Gerald McPherson. Poor Gerald lost his life more than a year ago, to a freak accident. He'd been in the forest felling trees with several other men. Unfortunately, Gerald cut one way, but the tree went another and he could not get away in time. The tree came crashing down, killing him instantly.

'Twas quite possible that Bhruic and Alyse knew each other.

But there was something in the way Alyse looked at Bhruic that told her it was much more than a mere acquaintance between them. She couldn't quite put her finger to it, but instinct told her there was more to it than even friendship.

In truth, it did not matter one way or another. Fiona was not going to marry Bhruic.

Fiona stood between Collin and William on the steps of their keep. They were watching the MacKinnon clan — the last of their visitors — leave through the gate. Relief washed over Fiona as the last mounted man went through.

"How did the MacKinnon take the news," William asked as he turned to face her.

"Better than I expected," Fiona said. "I thought fer certain he'd be quite angry, but he was no'. Though he does no' quite understand the way of a woman's heart, he was no' angry fer me turnin' down the offer."

Collin placed a hand on her shoulder and the three of them went inside. "Do ye think he'll remain an ally, even though he said no to marryin' his nephew?"

"Aye, I do." Though for the life of her she couldn't understand why. Something had happened over the past two days. Edgar had shown a less harsh side of himself, even after she told him she couldn't marry Bhruic. While she would not go so far as to call Edgar MacKinnon a friend, she now had a more positive attitude toward the man.

"Good," William said as they made their way through the gathering room and down the hallway to Fiona's office. "Lord knows we do no' need any more enemies."

"Were either of ye able to learn anythin' new?" Fiona asked.

Collin sighed and shook his head. "Unfortunately, no'. The only rumor that anyone speaks of now is that our water be magic. Ridiculous as that may seem."

"Water," Fiona said with a shake of her head. "All this over water. 'Tis as ludicrous as what William told me last night."

Collin paused just inside the study. "I fear I know no' of what ye speak," he said. Whilst he attempted to feign ignorance, his red face bespoke the truth. He knew exactly to what Fiona referred.

"Liar," Fiona said as she sat down behind her desk. "Ye ken *exactly* what I be speakin' of. That ridiculous story William told me last night. About how are mum was so worried over me stunnin' beauty that no one was ever to speak of it."

A knowing glance past between her brothers.

"Do ye truly expect me to believe it?" Fiona asked as she leaned forward in her seat.

With his eyes on his brother, William cast a slight motion of his head in Fiona's direction, as if to say *ye talk to her.*

Collin cleared his throat. "What William told ye be true."

Fiona stared at him. *Unbelievable.* After everyone had left her bedchamber the night before, she had thought a great deal about what William had told her. She was now thoroughly convinced that the stories had been made up, though the purpose of which evaded her. Believing that they felt sorry for their sister and only wanting to keep her from killing anyone who gave her a compliment, she had dismissed it all in its entirety.

"I appreciate what ye be tryin' to do," Fiona began as she folded her hands together and placed them on her desk. "But truly, 'tis no' necessary."

"Fi," Collin began before she cut him off.

"Collin, we've more important things to discuss than me beauty or lack thereof." Finished discussing the matter, she turned to William. "Have ye heard from Brodie?"

"Only that their healer is makin' him stay abed, much to his consternation," William said with a smile.

"It must be hell on earth fer him," Collin said. "He never was one to lay abed, unless he had someone *in* the bed with him."

Fiona laughed aloud. Brodie was definitely as fond of women as they were of him. But he was also a very proud man. "Does he say when he will be able to travel?"

"'Twill be at least two more weeks," William said. "That is, if he listens to the healer."

"I doubt he will listen to anyone," Fiona said. "Aside from complainin' about stayin' abed, does he have any new information fer us?"

William puffed his cheeks and let out a long breath. "Unfortunately, nay. Accordin' to everyone we've spoken to, this all be over water."

Fiona shook her head and pursed her lips together. "There has to be someone who kens more. Unfortunately, I do no' ken who that would be."

From the expressions on her brothers' faces, they were just as lost as she.

Eight

Young Conner McPherson had been having a most pleasant dream. One in which he was older and bigger and a warrior like his da and uncle Michael. He had a real sword, made from the finest steel. He was riding on the back of a fine black stallion, his father and uncle beside him. They were defending Scotland and their home.

"Conner! Maggie!" 'Twas his mum rousing him and his sister from their sleep. His mum sounded very upset and very afraid. "Wheesht!" she whispered harshly as she pulled first Conner from the pallet, then his wee sister. "Do no' say a word!" his mum whispered sharply as she led them to the little door in the wall that divided their sleeping loft from the barn loft attached to their hut.

"What's wrong?" Conner asked. He'd never seen his mum so afraid before. 'Twas still dark out, and only a sliver of moonlight shone into the one window in their loft.

"Wheesht, Conner," his mum said as she shoved him through the small door. His mum knelt down on one knee and shoved his sleepy sister in next. "Conner, no matter what ye hear, ye do no' leave the loft. Promise me, son, ye'll no' leave the loft."

Conner nodded his promise as his mum grabbed a blanket from his pallet and stuffed it through the door. "Remain as quiet as a mouse, Conner. Keep yer sister quiet too." He nodded again as he wrapped his arms around his little sister. 'Twas then that he heard loud voices coming in from out of doors. His mum heard them too and began to shut the tiny door. Before it closed all the way, she placed a kiss on her fingertips and touched first Conner's cheek, then Maggie's.

"If anythin' happens, Conner, ye go to the main keep. Ye've

been there before, remember? With yer da and yer uncle." His mum said as she held onto the door.

"Mum, I be afraid," Conner whispered. He would never have told his father that, because men were never afraid. He knew he could tell his mum for she always seemed to understand.

"I want me da," Maggie began to cry.

"Wheesht, now, my babes. I need ye to be as quiet as a wee mouse, no matter what happens, ye stay in this loft. In the morn, ye go to Collin McPherson."

"But why?" Conner asked as the voices grew louder and angrier and more frightening. He couldn't ever remember being this afraid, or seeing his mum in such distress before. His stomach began to feel sick, especially when the door closed. He and his sister were submerged into darkness.

"Conner," Maggie whispered softly, her little voice sounding very much afraid. "What is happenin'?"

He did not know for certain. The voices grew louder and angrier. He could not make out any words that were spoken for the wall between their living quarters and the barn would not allow it. That, and his heart was pounding so loudly he worried the angry voices would find them.

"Conner," Maggie whispered and trembled. "I want Da."

He wanted Da, too. He wanted the mean and angry sounding men to leave. He and Maggie nearly jumped from their skin when they heard a loud crash come from below stairs. It sounded like the front door had been kicked in. A moment later, they heard their mum screaming.

More crashing, more yelling and the sound of their mum's terrified shrieks filled the tiny space. Conner drew the blanket up and over his and Maggie's heads. Huddled under the blanket, they held onto one another for dear life, as if they were on a ship at sea fighting great waves as they tumbled through a storm.

The blanket only muffled the sounds that came from below. Their auld milk cow began to kick at the walls, lowing loudly while the chickens squawked frantically.

"Conner, I be scared," Maggie whispered as she clung to him, her little arms shaking, her chin quivering.

Supposing she might feel better if she knew he was also afraid, he said, "Me, too."

Being the oldest, it was up to him to keep his sister safe and out of trouble. How many times had his father said that to him? Conner had worn the title of big brother proudly, ever since Maggie had been born. For six years now, he'd done his best to keep her out of mischief and harm's way.

Now, as they were huddled under the blanket, hidden in darkness in the loft above the barn, he was uncertain he wanted to keep that title or those responsibilities. He didn't feel quite so brave or auld at the moment.

Still, he'd made his mum a promise and he'd do his best to keep it.

His mum screamed and screamed to the point that Conner was ready to scream himself. He had no idea what was happening below stairs nor what agony his mum was suffering that made her scream so loudly. Conner had Maggie cover her ears with her hands so that she could not hear it.

While he would have preferred not to listen, something in his belly told him he must. Listen closely, Conner. Wait until 'tis quiet and then ye can go to yer mum and help her.

Where was his da? Who were these strange men? He heard the high-pitched neighs of multiple horses and the pounding of hoofs on the ground. Conner strained his ears to listen. He thought he heard the horses running around the outer walls of their hut. Men were laughing, some shouted unintelligibly at what or who he was uncertain.

It seemed to Conner as if the ordeal went on for hours and hours, with him huddled under the blanket, holding on to his wee sister. More shouting, more laughter, his mother's screams. Suddenly, he felt like throwing up, but dared not for fear that whoever was below stairs tormenting his mother might hear him. Who knew what they'd do to him or to Maggie. Nay, he had to be brave and he had to be smart.

The cow grew increasingly agitated, as did the chickens, but it sounded as though the shouting and screaming had stopped.

Conner held his breath, strained his ears to listen, to hear over the cow and chickens and his ever-pounding heart. He waited. Finally, he dared take the chance to chance a peek from under the blanket.

The barn was still quite dark, barely any moonlight at all made its way into the space. When he finally let loose the breath he'd been holding, he caught the faint whiff of smoke.

Ever so carefully, he crawled from under the blanket and made his way to the edge of the loft. As he drew nearer, he could see something was glowing and flickering. When he made it to the edge, he could see the source of the orange glow.

The barn was on fire.

Though his mother had told him to wait until morn before he left the safety of the loft, the fire blazing in the corner below changed everything. Thinking quickly, he pulled the blanket away from his little sister.

"Maggie, do no' scream or cry. I need ye to listen to me."

She nodded her head and took his hand.

"The barn be on fire. We have to get out," he told her as he stood up and helped her to her feet. "Ye stay right behind me, Maggie. No matter what, do no' let go of me hand."

As she gave another nod, smoke began to billow up and into the loft. Conner knew they had to leave and leave quickly. He folded the blanket in half before wrapping it around Maggie's shoulders. She began to weep as she squeezed his hand tightly. "Conner, I be afraid! I want mum!"

"Wheesht now, Maggie," Conner said as he tried to sound brave and pretend that he knew what he was doing.

He tugged on the door and prayed no one below would hear him. He went through the door first, pulling Maggie behind him. Smoke followed from the barn into their loft. Uncertain what lay below or where his parents were, he pulled the door shut in hopes of keeping the smoke out of this portion of their home long enough to make an escape.

They crept to the edge of their loft and peered over the ledge. All the furniture below was askew, chairs broken and scattered about the room. Pots and dishes lay broken across the floor. Conner raced back to their pallet then and grabbed their boots. "Put yer boots on, Maggie," he whispered. "There be broken things below."

Maggie stood frozen with fear, unable to move. Conner tugged his boots on, then shoved Maggie's feet into hers. Smoke began to billow in through the cracks in the wall.

"Come, Maggie!" he said. "We must get out of here."

She didn't move.

"Maggie, please, we must hurry!"

She remained frozen in place. Conner felt like crying then. He wanted his mum, he wanted his da.

"Maggie, come, we must help Mum and Da!"

Hearing those words jolted her out of her fear induced trance and propelled her forward.

They scurried down the ladder, with Conner going first. He helped Maggie the rest of the way when his feet touched the stone floor. He glanced around the large room, but did not see either of his parents. Their little home was rapidly filling with smoke. Conner could hear the flames as they roared to life in the barn.

The door to their hut had been shattered and lay in bits on the floor. Carefully, holding on to Maggie's hand, he led them out of the hut and into the cold night air.

That's when he saw something so horrible it would be forever etched in his mind.

His father's lifeless body, covered in blood, was swaying to and fro from the wych elm tree not more than twenty yards ahead. His father's face was a terrifying shade of purple, his eyes staring at nothing whilst his tongue protruded through his open mouth.

Try as he might, Conner could not bring himself to look away. At first, he thought it too gruesome to be real. Mayhap 'twas all a bad dream.

Nay, if he were dreaming he would not be able to feel Maggie's cold clammy hand in his.

Maggie.

He had to protect her from the sickening sight of their father hanging dead from the tree. He spun around sharply and tugged the blanket over her head to shield her from it.

"I canna see!" Maggie argued.

"Wheesht!" Conner said, fighting back tears and a stomach that threatened to throw up its contents. He pulled her close and on trembling legs, he walked away from the hut and away from the tree. The cow screamed a most sickening sound. But he couldn't run it to free her for the barn was completely engulfed now.

Flames leapt from the barn and caught the thatched roof beside it aflame.

His voice was thoroughly lodged in his throat. Where was his mum? Panic welled and turned to tears as he looked around the yard for some sign of her. He really needed his mum.

Behind them, the fire roared. Though he could feel the heat coming from the flames, his insides felt as cold as the loch in winter time. He could feel Maggie more than hear her as she squeezed his hand and wept. "Where be mum?" she said over and over again.

They heard a loud booming sound coming from behind them. Together, they spun just in time to see the heavy wooden beams that used to be the roof to their barn, explode tumble down, imploding on itself.

Conner pulled Maggie away and began his frantic search for his mum.

Maggie saw her first.

She was lying face down in the mud some thirty yards away. He tried to stop Maggie from rushing to her, but her clammy hands were too slippery to hold on to. She pulled away and tore across the yard. "Mum!" she cried. "Mum!"

Conner ran after his sister. When he got closer, he could see the blood still oozing from his mum's bare back. Her face was bloodied, her lip cut, a large gash ran down the side of her face. Her bare back was scratched and cut and bruised. A large, gaping wound ran sideways, just under her left shoulder blade where blood had ceased to flow.

Maggie was trying to wake their mum, but Conner knew 'twas useless to try.

"Mum, please wake up," Maggie cried as she patted her back gently, as if she were afraid to hurt her. "Please mum, please."

Conner sank to his knees. For a long time, he felt numb all over.

"Mum, please wake up," Maggie said as she laid her tiny blonde head against her mother's back and continued to give her soft pats. Either she didn't notice or she refused to see the tremendous amount of her mother's blood she now knelt in. "Mum, I be afraid."

Tears began to run down Conner's cheeks. Everything was gone. His parents, their home, even their milk cow and chickens.

There was nothing left, but him and Maggie.

The realization made his stomach hurt and twist uncontrollably. He doubled over and wretched, vomit splattering against the mud.

Nine

Just after dawn, Fiona was roused from sleep by her brother, William. "There's been another raid," he seethed as he shook her awake.

Within short order, Fiona was dressed in tunic and trews and standing in her private study. Seamus and Andrew looked grief-stricken, whilst William looked mad enough to bite through iron.

"What happened?" Fiona asked, knowing full well she was not going to like the answers.

"A little over an hour ago, the night watch saw what appeared to be a large fire just east of here. They sent out scouts," William said, looking as distressed as he was angry. "'Twas Stephan and Mildred McPherson's croft."

Fiona's gut began to constrict. From William's red face, she felt certain that there was nothing good in what he was about to tell her.

"They were no' far from the croft when they came across wee Conner and Maggie, wanderin' in the dead of night, tryin' to make their way to the keep," William worked his jaw back and forth as he recounted what he'd been told. "They were covered in mud and tears, and blood."

Fiona's heart began to sink even further. Refusing to jump to any conclusions, she waited quietly for William to tell her all of it.

"A few of the scouts went on whilst two brought the children here."

Stephan and Mildred and their two children lived on the edge of McPherson lands, an hour's walk southwest of the keep. The children were young, a boy and a girl. If her memory served her correctly, they were between six and eight years of age.

"Where are they now?" Fiona asked as her heart pounded against her breast.

"Isabelle and Mairi have them," William said through gritted teeth. "One of our scouts returned a short while ago. Someone raided Stephan and Mildred's croft. They found Stephan hangin' from a tree..." his voice trailed off. He had to take a fortifying breath before he could continue on. "And Mildred," he choked on saying the poor woman's name.

Seamus stepped in to tell the rest of the story. "They found poor Mildred lyin' dead, face down in the mud."

Fury boiled deep within Fiona's stomach. Stephan and Mildred McPherson were two of the nicest people she'd ever known; their children were sweet and well-mannered. This went beyond a raid. This was a massacre of innocent lives.

"The lass will no' speak. She be the younger of the two," William said softly, visibly upset by the events.

Fiona found her voice and asked, "And what does the lad tell us?"

Seamus and Andrew cast each other a glance before Seamus answered. "He says his mum woke them in the middle of the night to hide them in the loft above the cow." Many of the crofters' huts shared space with the animals. Whilst the families lived in one side of the hut, they oft kept their milk cows and chickens in an attached barn. 'Twasn't always the best smelling of situations, but the arrangement was centuries old and quite convenient. Stephan and Mildred lived in such a hut.

"He says his mum was verra afraid, hurried them into the loft and bid them no' to make a sound," Seamus said. "They could no' see what was happenin', but they could hear. There were men on horses, how many he does no' ken, but the lad says it sounded like many. They could hear their da sayin' to the men they could take whatever they needed, but to leave his family be." Seamus swallowed hard and took a steadying breath before going further. "The lad says they could hear their parents bein' killed. Their mum screamin' fer mercy, their dad tryin' to fend off the raiders. The lad — his name be Conner by the way — said the hut grew quiet all of a sudden, then it began to fill with smoke."

Fiona felt her heart sink and her stomach contract further as she listened. *Those poor babes,* she thought to herself. Innocent children having to listen as their parents are slaughtered. The hell they must have gone through, the hell they most likely will have to endure the rest of their lives.

"As soon as the children arrived, Collin and Richard left with more scouts," William said.

Fiona felt her head begin to swim with visions of what Stephan and Mildred must have gone through, how terrified they all must have been.

"I'll no' make a decision until Collin returns. I will also need to speak with the children. Fer now, we'll let them rest. But I will have to question them." The thought of questioning two innocent and young children made her feel queasy.

"The lad is terribly distraught," Seamus said, clearly disgusted and angry. "I dunna ken how they managed to survive ..." his words trailed away as he paled visibly.

Fiona could not begin to imagine the hell that took place at that wee little farm. All she could think of at the moment was those poor little children.

Richard returned with three of the men a short time later. He stomped into Fiona's study, angrier than she'd ever seen him. His cheeks were covered in soot and sweat, his ginger hair all askew, and his green eyes aflame with barely controlled rage.

He walked straight to the side table, poured a large mug of whisky, and downed half of it before he was able to speak.

"We found Stephan hanging from a tree," he said before taking another long drink.

Fiona, Seamus and Andrew waited silently for Richard — who was visibly shaken — to work up the courage to tell them what he'd seen. They would not push for answers just yet.

"Mil —" he choked trying to get her name out. Clearing his throat, he began again. "Mildred ... they raped her before they killed her. She was lyin' face down in the mud, cut and scratched and beaten." He drank down the rest of his whisky before filling the mug again. "She'd never hurt a soul in her life. They raped her. They beat her. Then they stabbed her repeatedly and left her to die naked in the mud."

'Twas one thing to steal a few sheep. 'Twas quite another matter to kill innocent people. First Bridgett, now Stephan and Mildred McPherson. Three of the kindest people Fiona had ever known.

Fiona pushed to her feet as her rage bubbled to the surface. "All this because someone believes our water be magic?" she seethed, her voice loud and filled with anger. "Fer bloody water?"

Unable to contain her rage, she took her arm and swiped the contents from the top of her desk to the floor. "I'll no' stand fer this!" she shouted. "I'll no' cower. I'll no run. I'll no' hide. I will avenge their deaths. We will put an end to this, one way or another."

Collin and the scouts did not return for several hours. They had stayed behind to bury Stephan and Mildred.

Nothing was left behind that might indicate who was responsible for the senseless and brutal deaths. No *sgian dubhs,* no bits of plaid, no obvious message other than a burned home and two dead.

Collin was exhausted, his shoulders slumping as he sat in Fiona's study. They were alone now, just him and his sister. He had downed two tankards of ale before he had the courage to tell her what little he knew.

"From the hoof tracks we found, we think there were at least six men on horseback," he said in a low, steady voice. "I sent two men to follow. It appears they came in from the west and left in that same direction."

"It makes no sense," Fiona said as she sipped on her own mug of cider. "Why attack Stephan and Mildred? What could possibly be gained from it?" That question had been plaguing her from the start. *Why them?*

Collin shrugged his shoulders and shook his head. He was as baffled as anyone else. "I canna believe this be fer supposed magic water," he said. "There has to be more to it than that."

"I agree," Fiona said as she absentmindedly ran her finger around the rim of her mug. "But what?"

Collin sighed as he ran a hand through his hair. "I dunna ken, Fiona, I dunna ken."

They sat in quiet contemplation for some time before Collin

spoke again. "What do we do now?"

'Twas another question she could not answer fully. "We bring all of our people in. Send riders out immediately to warn them. We have less than a dozen crofters throughout our lands. Bring them all inside the walls. Our livestock as well," she stood and went to the door and opened it. Two young lads had been standing outside her study waiting. Fiona pointed to each lad, "Run and fetch William and Seamus lads. Tell them I need them at once." The boys gave a nod before running off to do as she'd asked.

Shutting the door, she returned to her place across from Collin and sat. "Ye look like hell," she told him. Dark circles surrounded his blue eyes, his hair was disheveled, and a smudge of dirt lined his left jaw. His clothes were filthy and smelled of smoke.

Collin smiled. "I could say the same of ye."

"We've no' had much sleep these past weeks," Fiona remarked. "I fear we'll no' be gettin' much more until we find out who is responsible for these raids and murders."

Collin took a long pull on his ale. "We need more men and weapons," he said as he stared at the half empty mug.

Fiona knew where he was going with that statement. "Aye, we do."

He looked up at her through heavy lids. "Have ye made a decision?" he asked, referring to Edgar MacKinnon's proposal.

"Nay, I've no'." Until she'd been woken to the news of Stephan and Mildred's murders, she had believed she had made up her mind. She was not going to marry Bhruic. But these new murders, this senseless and brutal raid had put things in a new and quite harsh light.

"Fiona, I ken ye do no' love Bhruic," Collin began. "Under normal circumstances, I'd no' press ye to do anythin' ye do no' wish to do."

She remained quiet and listened. She knew he was not going to tell her anything she hadn't been thinking about for the past few hours.

"I fear we will no' be able to defend ourselves, Fiona. Especially if this be someone from a much larger clan. Our men, while we've trained them well, they be no' used to battle. Hell, a good majority of them have never even seen battle. While I trust their fealty and determination, that alone might no' be enough when the time comes."

Fiona let out a long, slow breath. Every word of what her brother said was true. He neither exaggerated nor did he try to make things seem less than they were.

"We've no one else to go to fer help, Fiona, save fer the McDunnahs. Fer now, they be the only clan that I truly trust."

Fiona wondered if she were to go to Caelen for help, would he give it? Considering how she'd left him days before, she seriously doubted it. And she could not rightly blame him. "I fear Caelen will no' help us now."

Collin raised a brow. "I do no' agree. He's an honorable man, Fiona. He'd help if ye'd let him."

"Caelen asked me to marry him, Collin. I told him nay." She let a few moments pass, allowing what she'd finally admitted aloud to settle in.

"Why?" Collin asked as he studied her closely.

"Why do ye think?" she asked, exasperated. "If I were to marry Caelen, our clan would be absorbed into theirs. I promised James, his father and ours that I'd never allow that to happen."

"Would that be so bad?" Collin asked.

Fiona's eyes widened with shock. "Are ye daft? Of course 'twould be bad! I'd be breakin' me word. I'll no' go crawlin' away from me word, from me oath at the first hint of troubles!" Mayhap 'twas exhaustion that made Collin ask such a thing, mayhap 'twas madness, or mayhap 'twas frustration. Either way, it did not matter. Fiona would die before she'd ever consider doing such a thing.

"Then ye'll consider marryin' Bhruic?" Collin finally asked. "Fer our clan?"

There was no way around it. "Aye, I'll consider it."

"We may no' have much time fer you to linger on it, Fiona."

She glared at him. "I ken that, Collin!"

"I wish things could be different, Fiona. But ye knew the day ye took yer oath as chief that ye'd have to face some verra difficult decisions."

She snorted derisively. "Aye, but I never imagined anythin' like what I face now."

The McPherson scouts returned late in the afternoon. Covered with mud and muck, they rode through the gates and hurried into the keep in search of Collin and Fiona.

Fiona had heard the call to raise the gates and entered the gathering room from her study. Collin came bounding down the stairs at the same time. He'd managed to bathe and catch an hour's worth of sleep.

Drigh McPherson had led the scouting party. He now stood before Fiona, looking tired and frustrated. "We followed west as far as we could, clear to the border with the MacElroys," he was out of breath, travel-worn and weary. "The tracks then turned south, but the rains washed away any further signs, Fiona. We lost them." He sounded dejected.

MacElroys, Fiona thought. Could the MacElroy be behind all of this? Was he arrogant enough or insane enough to do such a thing? "But they did no' cross onto MacElroy land?"

Drigh gave a shake of his head. "No' that we could tell. Again, there was too much mud to tell where they went after turnin' south."

Fiona thanked the men. "Go, bathe and eat and get some rest," she told them.

"I be terribly sorry, Fiona," Drigh said with sagging shoulders.

"Do no' worry over it," Fiona told him. "Ye've done as good as ye could under the circumstances. Now go, do as I said. Rest up, fer I may need ye to ride again."

The men gave cursory bows before quitting the gathering room.

Collin came to stand beside her, looking as confused and as concerned as Fiona felt.

"Do ye think it could be the MacElroy?"

"In truth, Collin, I do no' ken. It could be another ruse, like with the McDunnahs. It could be they only want us to think he be responsible."

Collin gave that some thought for a moment. "True, but we canna take any chances."

He was right. The MacElroy clan was much bigger than her own, its men far more seasoned when it came to border wars and battles. She did not know if her own small clan would be able to stand up to them, though they'd certainly do their best to try. And what if the MacElroy did not act alone? What if it was more than just one clan at fault?

The odds were sorely against them.

In that small moment of time, she knew what she must do. She would marry Bhruic MacKinnon.

Ten

The following few days seemed to drag on endlessly for Caelen as he waited both for Nial and Bree's arrival and word from Angus' spies. He knew it could be weeks before anyone returned with any news, but still, the wait was exhausting.

Though 'twas good to be back at Castle Gregor and spending time with his old friends, he missed his own home. Most of all, he missed Fiona.

He worried for her. Was she safe? Did she miss him? Were Collin and William watching over her, keeping her both out of harm's way and out of trouble? Her brother Brodie was still recuperating from his wounds at Caelen's keep. Brodie had wanted to join Caelen in his journey to the MacDougalls but their healer, an ancient man name Marlich, had refused to allow it. According to Brodie, his brother William fancied himself Fiona's protector. Caelen could only pray that Brodie was right and William would do whatever he could to keep Fiona safe.

He had slept through the evening meal on his first night at the MacDougalls. The second night, however, his friends Duncan and Wee William made certain he would not miss the evening festivities. The two men all but dragged him into the grand gathering room.

While he was quite happy that his friends had found solace and comfort in their beautiful wives, happy that the good Lord had blessed them with far too many children to count, he admittedly hated them for it. Not vehemently nor with a soul-crushing passion. Nay, he was simply envious and that 'twas an entirely new experience for him.

He'd never envied anyone for anything. He happily went about his life, doing his best to avoid holding other people's babes, ignoring the fact that he was getting aulder and lonelier and far less likable.

Fiona had changed all that. Now, when he looked at Wee William and Nora, or Duncan and Aishlinn, or Angus and Isobel, he felt nothing short of envious which in turn left him quite despondent.

He lay in bed each night and tried to cipher it all out. How had he come to be so hopelessly in love with Fiona McPherson? He hadn't been looking for love, quite the contrary. He'd avoided it at all costs.

He hadn't thought he'd been lonely, until she came into his life. He hadn't been looking or seeking anything more than a quick tumble betwixt the sheets with women whose names he cared not to know.

Now? Now he had travelled for two days, fought rain and wind to get here, to seek the help of old friends. Now, he lay in bed at night, questioning his own sanity.

He would have loved to have the energy and wherewithal to curse Fiona McPherson for turning his life upside down. He couldn't blame her, for he knew she hadn't intentionally set out to steal his heart or to break it.

There was no one to blame but himself. He'd let his guard down, let the stone walls he'd erected around his heart to crack wide enough to allow that spark of love to enter.

He was a bloody fool.

No matter the whys or the wherefores, he was in a sad and sorry state. He couldn't bear to think of what would happen to him, to his very soul, if he could not find a way to marry her, to spend every day of the rest of his life with her.

Aye, he was a complete, utter, bloody fool.

As soon as Caelen had received word that Nial and Bree were not far away, he raced down the stairs and out of the keep to wait in the courtyard for their arrival. He and Nial had been friends for many years. They'd fought side by side in many a battle against the English, in border wars, and aye, even a few tavern brawls.

Caelen couldn't recount the number of times Nial had saved his neck, but knowing his friend as he did, Nial would be able to recount each and every one of them.

They were as opposite as two people could be. While Nial preferred to negotiate his way out of difficult situations, Caelen preferred a more straightforward approach, by using his fists or his sword. Where women swooned over Nial's tall, handsome physique they tended to stay clear of Caelen.

Nial led some thirty McKee warriors, half of whom were surrounding his lovely wife Bree, through the gates and into the courtyard.

Nial pulled rein on his brown and white gelding, slid from his horse and went straight to his old friend. The two men shook arms and embraced, slapping each other hard on their backs. "What trouble have ye gotten yerself into now?" Nial asked as he pulled away to scrutinize Caelen.

Bree, just as beautiful as she'd always been, slid from her own mount, smoothed out the wrinkles on her dark red gown and walked toward her husband. "Thank ye kindly, husband fer helpin' me down from me horse. 'Twas much appreciated."

Nial rolled his eyes at Caelen before turning his attention to his wife. "Did ye struggle much in gettin' down?"

Bree rolled her bright green eyes and elbowed her husband in his ribs before going to Caelen. Giving him a warm hug she said, "Ignore him, Caelen. He's cranky because he had to sleep out of doors last night. He's grown too soft these past years."

Nial pretended to grab an imaginary dagger from his heart. "Ye wound me wife, ye wound me."

Bree ignored him and draped an arm through Caelen's, lifted her dress in one dainty hand and began to head up the steps. "I fear me husband has lost his mind, Caelen."

"Bah! I didna lose it, wife, ye stole it from me!" Nial said playfully from behind.

Bree shook her head as if she was truly despaired. "He was no' usin' it anyway."

Caelen had to laugh at the playful back and forth that Nial and Bree shared with one another. While they might pretend to fuss and grumble and complain about the other, no one believed it for a minute. They genuinely loved each other as evidenced by the six children they had created together.

They made their way up the steps, into the keep and into the grand gathering room. Food and refreshments were being brought in. As Caelen was escorting Bree to the table, her mother, Isobel, came floating eagerly down the stairs. "Bree!" she exclaimed with a bright happy smile.

Hearing her mum's voice, a beautiful smile exploded on Bree's face as she raced to greet her mother. The two started talking so rapidly and with such excitement that it was difficult for Caelen to keep up.

Nial chuckled as he took a seat at the table. "They'll be that way fer hours, Caelen. It has been at least six months since last they saw one another."

Caelen looked on rather amused by the spectacle. Without so much as a by-your-leave, the two women ascended the stairs and disappeared.

"Aye," Nial said as he poured himself a mug of ale. "They be like that every time they see one another."

Caelen shrugged his shoulders and sat down across from his friend. "I'll never understand the opposite sex."

Nial chuckled. "I fear no man ever will, my friend." Grabbing a wooden plate, he began cutting pieces of cheese and meat and carefully placing them on the plate. After several long moments of silence, he finally looked up at Caelen.

"So tell me what trouble ye've found and what can I do to help."

Caelen took a deep, cleansing breath. While he searched for a way to explain the events of the past few weeks in a way that wouldn't make him look like a besotted fool, Nial studied him closely.

The silence stretched on. No matter what road he took to try to explain his predicament, he realized he could not do it without explaining how he felt about Fiona McPherson. The ribbing and teasing he would receive from Nial would be ruthless and never-ending. He felt his face warm and turn red under Nial's close scrutiny.

"My God," Nial finally said with his mouth agape. "Ye've fallen in love!" He threw his head back and laughed heartily.

Months ago, Nial's laughter would have been a good excuse for

Caelen to knock him on his arse. But now? He couldn't, for Nial spoke only the truth. Still, it irked Caelen that Nial was taking so much enjoyment out of his unease.

"Well, welcome to the human race, my friend," Nial said after he reined in his laughter. He held up his mug of ale and toasted the air between them. "It be about bloody time."

Eleven

'Twas the last thing in this world that she wanted to do — marry someone other than Caelen. Fiona felt she was doing what any chief worth her weight in barley would have done; sacrificed her personal life for the life and future of her clan. There was no other way.

Though Collin and William were glad she had made the decision, if only for the sake of their clan, Fiona knew they felt some measure of guilt, sadness and even a little anger. Guilt that it had to be she who made the sacrifice for the greater good. Sadness for they knew her heart was not in it. And anger toward whoever was behind the raids and murders.

Would that they could change the facts and circumstances around Fiona's upcoming nuptials, but alas, there was naught that could be done for it. Therefore, they all met with Edgar and Bhruic on a rainy Highland morning, in Fiona's study, to hash out the details. Fiona and her brothers sat facing Edgar and Bhruic. If her intuition was correct, Bhruic was not nearly as thrilled with the prospect of marriage as Edgar was.

They'd make an ideal pair, she and Bhruic. Miserable companions who would paint smiles on their faces and live out the rest of their days pretending they were happy.

Collin read aloud from the scroll before him. "In exchange for the marriage between Fiona McPherson and Bhruic MacKinnon, Clan MacKinnon agrees to provide no' less than one-hundred battle-ready men, three wagons of barley, one wagon of wheat, and the promise of aid in the future should the need arise." Collin glanced up from the scroll, his eyes locked with Fiona's for a brief moment. With a nod, she signified her agreement. He continued, "It is furthermore agreed in good faith, that Clan McPherson shall provide no less than six kegs of their finest whisky at Hogmanay for the next six years. From this day forward, McPherson and MacKinnon shall be considered kith and kin with all the rights and privileges such brings with it. They shall be allies and agree ne'er to raise arms agin each other."

There it was. In writing. Her future, all laid out neatly and tidily, just as it had happened nine years ago. Though in truth, she *had* been happy about her marriage to James. Oh, she knew he didn't truly love her, but her naive sixteen-year-old self believed that he *could* and that was all that mattered.

Now, she was aulder, wiser, and far more cynical than she had been in her youth. Long ago, she had believed in the kind of love that bards sang about. After years of disappointment and a husband who could not love her, she quit believing in such things. They were nothing more than fairy tales meant to give young women hope when they embarked on their life's mission of being a wife and mother. Ghosts, brownies and fairies were more real than romantic love.

A sennight ago, she discovered that yes, true, passionate and undying love did exist. 'Twas quite real. Real enough that her heart felt ripped from her chest while one hundred horses trampled it into the cold, hard earth.

As she sat at the table and listened to the men around her barter over her future and the future of her clan, she could not decide which was worse. Owning a heart of stone that did not believe in those old fairy tales or owning one that knew they were more than stories.

The only thing that kept her from running out of the room screaming like a banshee was the knowledge that countless lives would be saved by this union. She and Bhruic were nothing more than sacrificial lambs, heading to the slaughter.

"If yer agreeable," Edgar said, unable to hide the glee in his eyes, "we'll post the banns fer a sennight?"

Believing there was no point in trying to avoid the inevitable, Fiona agreed. "That will be fine."

So it was written, so it was done.

Twelve

"I told ye to keep to that bed fer another fortnight," the auld healer, Marlich barked.

Brodie ground his teeth together, as he stood next to the small window, sorely tempted to throw the auld man out of it. "And I told ye that I canna stay in that bed another day. I'm no' a bairn with the ague or the pox."

"Bah!" Marlich said as he threw his hands up in the air. "Ye may no' have the ague or the pox, but yer behavin' like a spoilt bairn just the same. Ye'll lose that leg of yers if ye do no' listen to me words."

"I've been in that bed fer a fortnight now and I'll no' stay in it one day longer!"

Marlich shook his head and headed to the door. "Verra well then, but when the leg becomes festered I shall take great pleasure in usin' a dull, jagged knife to cut it from ye!"

As he went to lift the latch, a knock came at the door. Marlich lifted it and flung it open, fed up with Brodie's obstinate refusal to listen to his advice. Standing in the doorway was Marlich's oldest granddaughter, Nola. A comely lass with long dark hair and brown eyes. Marlich had been teaching her everything he knew about the healing arts and she had been helping him tend to Brodie. She was the one person in the world who could soften the auld man's temper.

"Grandda," she said, looking quite concerned as she stepped into the small room. "What be the matter?"

"Bah! The fool will no' listen to me," Marlich said. "He be

refusin' to listen to me."

Nola's hands went to her hips as she scrutinized Brodie closely for a long moment. "No worries, Grandda. I'll keep Brodie company whilst ye go find cousin Aric, the carpenter. He be verra good at makin' coffins as well as wooden legs. We'll know by the end of tomorrow which one Brodie shall need."

Brodie rolled his eyes. Marlich smiled proudly. "Verra well then, lass. I'll leave the heathen to ye."

Nola watched her grandfather leave the room. As soon as he shut the door behind him, she turned to Brodie. "Why will ye no' listen to him? He only means to see that ye do no' lose yer leg or yer life."

Brodie crossed his arms over his chest and stared down at the young woman. With Fiona McPherson as his sister, he was used to stubborn and intelligent women. "I be no' some bairn that needs lookin' after."

Nola mirrored him by crossing her arms over her own chest. "Nay, yer worse. Yer a stubborn, pig-headed man. I'd rather tend to a hundred cranky bairns than one injured man any day of the year."

"Then mayhap ye should leave me be and go tend to someone who needs it," he told her quite bluntly.

Nola was unfazed by his attempt to be rude. "Why will ye no' listen? What be so wrong with restin' until yer leg is completely healed?"

He glared at her. "Me leg is fine and I be verra tired of layin' about all the day long."

Nola raised one delicate eyebrow. "Fine, is it?" she asked. "Verra well. Walk with me."

He knew she was testing him on purpose. The wound had healed nicely as far as he was concerned. It hadn't turned red or festered and neither had he suffered with fevers. Nola and Marlich had done an excellent job at tending to it. However, the wound still pained him, causing him to limp slightly when he walked. But if it was a battle of wills that she wanted, he saw no reason to deny her.

Brodie pushed away from the wall he'd been leaning against and went to stand before her. He gave her the most dashing bow he could manage and flashed his most brilliant swoon-worthy smile. "Are ye happy?" he asked.

Nola quirked her brow and rested one hand on her hip. "With three steps?" she asked with a tilt of her head. "Nay, I be no' impressed by three steps. Me wee nephew can walk that far and he be only eight months auld."

Brodie McPherson was never one to back down from a challenge. "So, ye want me to walk more than three steps? I thought ye wanted me to lie abed until I be ninety."

"I ne'er said that, me grandda did. If 'twere up to me, ye'd have been walkin' a sennight ago and out of me hair."

"Might I remind ye," Brodie said as he leaned down to look her in the eye, "that I've repeatedly asked fer a horse so that I could return home?"

Nola did not shy away from his close proximity. "And I told ye that all ye had to do was get yerself to the stables and take one."

"And be accused of horse reivin'?" he asked. "I think no'."

"Caelen would no' accuse ye of such and ye ken it. Would ye like me to go and fetch ye one? Bring it above stairs here to yer room? Ye can stand on me back to mount it if ye've a need."

It angered Brodie to no end that Nola had been correct. By the time they made their way back into the keep, he would have sworn someone was jabbing his injury with a hot poker.

Thankfully, Nola remained quiet and did not dispense any *I told ye sos.* Instead, she graciously helped him up the stairs, standing off to the side but kept a steadying hand on his waist.

"Ye may lean on me if ye wish, Brodie," she told him in a soft, tender voice.

For reasons he couldn't quite fathom, he felt he'd rather have his leg cut off than to ask this slip of a woman for any kind of assistance. Through gritted teeth, he replied, "I be fine." He also could not fathom why he was irritated with her for she was only being kind.

Just two steps before the top of the landing his leg, weak from all the walking and burning like hell itself, buckled and gave out. Had it not been for Nola, he could very well have cracked his head on the stone stairs.

As soon as his leg gave out, he pitched forward, but before he could fall flat on his face, Nola lunged in front of him, wrapped her arms around his waist and held on tightly. She landed on her bottom before ending up prone against the stairs. Brodie landed with his face planted against her bosom.

He felt his face burn red with humiliation as he lifted his head and looked up. Nola's eyes were as wide as trenchers as her cheeks turned a delightful shade of pink.

"Are ye hurt?" he finally managed to ask.

"Nay," she said in a soft whisper.

"I be terribly sorry," Brodie said though he still hadn't made any effort to remove himself.

Nola seemed frozen in place as she continued to stare at him.

She be quite bonny, Brodie thought, when she be no' naggin' him about his leg.

Another long moment passed before he realized he needed to remove his person from hers. As he lifted himself up and away, Nola sighed, either with relief or regret, he could not be certain. He preferred to think it was the latter.

As Brodie leaned against her, Nola pushed open the door to his room and helped him to sit on the bed. "Lie back and let me check yer leg," she said as she lifted his good leg up and spun him around as if he weighed no more than a feather. Caught off once again by her physical strength — or his own lack thereof — he fell back on the bed with an humph. Pain coursed up and down his leg, making him instantly angry. "Are ye tryin' to kill me?"

Nola smiled. "Nay, I be tryin' to help."

She sat on the side of the bed and pushed his plaid up, just enough to afford her a glance at his injury. "It be fine," she announced before pulling the plaid back over his thigh.

"Fer a healer, ye've the bedside manner of a drunkard forced into sobriety."

Nola stood up and glared at him. "First ye do no' want me help, swear ye do no' need to be coddled like a babe, swear yer fine and can walk with no troubles, and curse me again fer helpin' ye. Now, ye complain I'm no' nice enough?" She shook her head in disbelief. "Yer a confusin' man, Brodie McPherson. I pity the woman unlucky enough to be yer wife someday. Ye'll drive her daft within a week."

Brodie scoffed at her assessment. "There be where yer wrong fer if the day ever arrives that I do marry, 'twill be a quiet, sweet, amiable lass. Not some cold-hearted shrew such as ye!"

He saw it then, a flicker of pain in her wide, brown eyes. It was fleeting, just a flash really, before he caught just a glimpse of sadness before they turned to fire with fury. He'd crossed the line from complaint to insult, a line he should not have crossed.

If he were to admit the truth, it wasn't Nola he was angry with, but himself. He was still embarrassed that he'd fallen from his horse. He prided himself in his excellent horsemanship skills. To be thrown from his mount was humiliation enough. To be thrown and injured so severely was mortifying.

"Curse ye, Brodie McPherson." Her voice was steady, calm, and low. "I hope the good Lord curses ye with a loud, mean wife who is just as arrogant and obnoxious as ye."

He was about to apologize to her when the door to his room flew open and Phillip stepped inside. "We need to talk."

From the look on his face, Brodie sensed the man was about to deliver him bad news.

"I'll leave ye be," Nola said as she headed toward the door.

Phillip reached out and touched her arm. "Nay, ye may stay, Nola." His eyes pleaded with her to remain. Against her better judgment, she looked over her shoulder at Brodie for his opinion. He swallowed hard before giving her a slight nod.

Nola sat on the small stool by the bed and folded her hands in her lap. From the corner of his eye, Brodie could see that she was angry with him. Why she chose to remain instead of kicking him in his bloody stubborn arse was an amazement unto itself. He didn't deserve her kindness, but he'd be glad for it all the same.

"I've just received messages from Collin," Phillip began, looking quite serious. "There was another raid on yer lands, Brodie."

Brodie sat forward, the action bringing about a deep ache in his thigh. Wincing, he asked for clarification.

"Six or more men, two nights past. They killed two of yer people. Stephan and Mildred McPherson."

His chest constricted tightly. He'd known Stephan and Mildred his whole life. "What of their children?" he asked, afraid to know the answer.

"The children are alive and stayin' at the keep. Yer family is takin' care of them, but that is all I know on that matter."

Brodie let loose with a sigh of relief in hearing that at least the children lived. He refused to allow his mind to wonder what they might have gone through. "Be there more?"

Phillip looked first to Nola then to Brodie. He shifted from one foot to the next as if there was worse news than two dead friends. "Aye, and I be glad that Caelen be no' here to hear it."

Brodie raised a curious brow. "What could possibly be so bad that ye'd no' want Caelen to hear it?"

Phillip cleared his throat before answering. "It has to do with yer sister."

Fear began to bubble up from the pit of his stomach. "Fiona? Is she injured? Ill? What be the matter?" he asked anxiously.

"Apparently, she's set to marry Bhruic MacKinnon in five days' time."

Brodie swung his feet over the edge of the bed and stood so quickly that he nearly fell onto Nola. "Who the bloody hell is Bhruic MacKinnon?" he shouted.

Phillip took a step back. "Apparently the nephew of Edgar MacKinnon."

He was beyond confused. Fiona loved Caelen, he knew that and without a doubt, Caelen loved her. Why on earth was she doing something so foolish as to marry someone else? His mind reeled, wholly dumbfounded at this turn of events. "Are ye certain it be Fiona marryin'?"

"Her name be on the banns," Phillip said. "Be there another Fiona McPherson?"

Brodie blew out a frustrated breath. "Nay, there be only one Fiona McPherson. And she be a fool if she thinks I'll allow her to marry this Bhruic MacKinnon!" He began to pace, as much as the tight confines of the room would allow. "Why on earth are Collin and William allowin' this?" he asked aloud to no one in particular.

"Mayhap she loves him," Nola offered.

The two men looked at her as if she had no sense at all. "Nay, lass, she does no' love him," Phillip told her.

"Well how do ye ken?"

Phillip sighed. "Because she loves Caelen."

'Twas Nola's turn to look confused. "Then why marry Bhruic?"

"Ye've no' yet had the pleasure of meetin' me sister, have ye?" Brodie asked.

"Nay," Nola admitted. "But I've heard she be a fierce warrior."

"Aye, she be fierce with sword and knife alike," Brodie said with a smile. "But she be also the most stubborn woman I've ever met in me life."

Nola drew in her lips to stem a smile and compose herself before asking sarcastically, "More stubborn than me even?"

Brodie drew his brows in and glared at her. "Aye, even more than ye." He turned his attention back to Phillip. "Was there any reason as to *why* Fiona has decided to marry this man?"

Phillip shook his head, "Nay, Brodie, no explanation, just the banns."

He began to wonder what else he had missed out on whilst recuperating at the McDunnah keep. Certainly his brothers could not be in support of Fiona's decision. Mayhap they were now working to get her to change her mind. Hope was probably futile. Once his sister made up her mind, 'twas next to impossible to get her to change it.

Phillip looked to Nola. "Can he ride?" he asked with a gesture toward Brodie. "He may want to get back to his keep."

Before Nola could say aye or nay on the matter, Brodie spoke up. "I'll no' be goin' to my keep," he told them.

While Phillip looked perplexed, Nola looked relieved.

"I would no' be able to change her mind," Brodie said.

"This will kill Caelen," Phillip muttered.

"Mayhap," Brodie said.

As Brodie saw it, he only had one clear choice.

He would not go home to the McPherson keep for he knew the chances were good that he'd not be able to talk his sister out of marrying Bhruic MacKinnon. Trying to talk his sister into or out of anything was pointless, especially if her mind was made up. Now, that wasn't to say she could not be persuaded to see different points of view. But if she firmly believed her decision was based for good and just reasons, there was no changing her mind.

Therefore, his only option was to get to MacDougall lands, give Caelen the news and hope that the man would be mad enough to put a stop to the wedding. If he knew Caelen as well as he thought he did, then he was making the right decision in going there and not back home.

Only one obstacle stood in his way and it came in the form of a wee lass with dark hair and brown eyes, which, after closer inspection from their earlier fall on the stairs, had little flecks of gold in them. Nola.

"I do no' understand why ye'd risk yer leg, if no' yer life by traipsin' all that way when ye could just as easily send a messenger." She was standing between him and the door, her feet firmly planted, her determination resolute.

"Nola, I do appreciate your concern on the matter," he tried explaining his reasoning to her, but she cut him off.

"Nay, fer if ye did appreciate me advice or me concern, ye'd get back in that bed and stay there."

"Nola, I be neither yer prisoner nor yer hostage. I do no' need yer permission to do anythin', now please, step aside and let me pass."

She continued to stare up at him and refused to move aside.

"Nola, this be far too important a matter to leave to a mere messenger. Me sister's entire future be at stake."

"Ye do no' ken *why* she be marryin' the man, so why do ye feel ye must stop her? Ye make no sense."

He was growing frustrated with her obstinance. 'Twas truly none of her business why he was doing what he was doing.

"Nola, I'll no' stand her any longer wastin' valuable time tryin' to get ye to understand me reasons fer goin'. Me sister loves Caelen and he loves her and right now, that be all that matters."

As if that somehow made sense, her full pink lips formed an 'o' shape and sudden understanding lit in her eyes. "Ye be a romantic. I would never have guessed that about ye, Brodie McCray," she said as if she were greatly impressed with him. She stepped aside then, to let him pass.

"Thank ye, Nola," he said, relieved she'd given up on the idea of trying to stop him.

"I hope ye will be able to find ye a sweet, kind woman to marry someday."

Believing she'd just offered an olive branch, Brodie smiled and bowed. "I thank ye kindly, Nola. And I wish fer ye a kind, good man someday."

She smiled sweetly. "Hopefully that sweet kind woman will no' care that yer missin' a leg."

'Twas quite difficult to maintain his composure when the woman seemed hell-bent on infuriating him. He could have said any number of mean-spirited, spiteful, or rude things. Instead, he surprised even himself, by going to her and leaning in so close to her, that he could see her pulse throbbing happily in the vein of her very delicate neck.

"Trust me, lass. My wife will no' care about a missin' leg, fer I'll be too busy pleasin' her in our marital bed."

He pulled away to see her wide eyed and stunned, he believed, due to his provocative statement. Just before he left the room, he bowed graciously and smiled deviously. 'Twas the first time since he'd met her that she'd been speechless.

Phillip needed very little convincing from Brodie that someone needed to inform Caelen of the banns. Within an hour of receiving the news, Brodie was on his way to the MacDougall keep, with fifteen McDunnah men. While Brodie road east, Phillip made plans to leave for McPherson lands in two days time. He had one simple order; if Brodie and Caelen had not arrived at the McPherson keep before the wedding began, Phillip was to delay it by any means necessary.

As he watched Brodie and the other men leave, Phillip sent up a silent prayer. He seriously doubted he'd be able to keep Fiona McPherson from doing anything.

Thirteen

The entire McPherson keep was a whirlwind of excitement as they prepared for the wedding between Fiona and Bhruic. The kitchen was abuzz with people chatting excitedly as they made all manner of baked goods, meats, fruits — another meal fit for a king.

Fiona, however, was unable to find within herself even an inkling of good cheer. The best she could do was paint a smile on her face to hide the misery in her heart.

Everything she now did was for the betterment and safety of her clan. She would gain nothing from this marriage other than the sense of security in knowing she would have more than one hundred additional skilled fighting men and the chance to call Bhruic's daughter hers.

After signing the agreement and posting the banns, Fiona merely went through the motions of pretending she cared one whit about any of it. She allowed Isabelle and Mairi to make all the arrangements. The only caveat was that they could not spend all the gold in their coffers. Other than that, her sisters-in-law were given free-rein to choose everything from the food that would be served to the gown she would wear.

While the days might have flown by for everyone else, they trudged on for Fiona at a snail's pace. Sleep evaded her as if she were the devil incarnate. On those rare occasions when she did manage to doze off, her dreams were plagued with images of Caelen or Bridgett or Stephan and Mildred, and if not any of them, the two children left behind.

The day before the wedding finally arrived and she could find no peace within the walls of her keep. The air was stifling, the clamor and excitement of her people preparing for a wedding roared in her ears. No matter which room she tried to hide away in, someone would come running with a multitude of questions for which she either had no answer or simply didn't care.

With the noise and commotion at a fevered pitch, Fiona had reached the end of her patience. Donning a cloak, she attempted to make her way through the front of the keep. As soon as people realized she was present, they swarmed like bees around a hive. "Ask Mairi or Isabelle," was her pat response to any question thrown her way.

In the end, she could reach neither the front door nor the back without being barraged with questions or well-wishes. After several failed attempts, she did the only sensible thing remaining. She went to her study, barred the door, and slipped out through the window. Unfortunately her study was on the main floor and there was no hope for a long fall that would break her neck. She escaped through the window without so much as a scratch.

Pulling the hood of her cloak over her head, she stealthily made her way around the side of the keep and headed for her mountain. 'Twas her fervent hope that no one would think to look for her there. And if they did, she had the option of jumping to her death. 'Twould be worth it just for a few moments of peace and solitude.

Keeping to the outer wall, she made her way to the stones that her people had been using for centuries to climb *Sidh Chailleann.* The going was not nearly as treacherous as she would have preferred on this solemn day before her wedding. The rain had stayed away and the sun was doing a fine job at keeping the earth warm and dry. What she wouldn't give for a torrential storm, a bolt of lightning, a huge gust of wind.

Mayhap all the stories of brownies and fairies her mother had plied her with in her youth were true and one of them would appear to take her away. Nay, she realized, she was not that lucky.

She made her way to the very ledge she had shared with Caelen weeks ago. She sat, as she had then, with her feet dangling over the edge, and looked down upon her home. Too many people to count flittered about below. The MacKinnons hadn't left since the day they had arrived to arrange the marriage. Whilst Edgar was given a room indoors, the rest of his people made camp inside and outside the walls.

Yesterday, MacElroy the Arrogant had arrived along with

dozens of his people. The McGregors followed not long after. The McKenzies and Farquars were due to arrive later. She prayed they'd all be thoughtful and bring their own food, the greedy sots.

"Ye've got to pull yerself out of this, Fiona," she murmured aloud. Didn't people say that one of the first signs someone had lost their mind was when they began to talk to themselves? "Ye canna continue on this morose path, all sullen and full of despair. Ye knew when ye took yer oath that someday ye'd have to face some verra difficult decisions. Ye knew ye might have to sacrifice yer own happiness for the good of yer clan."

Knowing the possibilities existed was nothing compared to actually having to live through them.

There was nothing to be done for it. Tomorrow she would don whatever monstrously revealing gown Isabelle and Mairi had come up with and she would walk into their wee kirk and exchange vows with Bhruic MacKinnon. She would do it with grace and dignity. She would do it for her clan.

When she dared not risk staying any longer, Fiona carefully made her way down the mountain and back inside the walls of her keep. After chastising herself for behaving so poorly — for it was, after all her own decision to marry Bhruic — she felt marginally better.

She would marry Bhruic, but her heart would always belong to Caelen. In it, tucked away and hidden, she would keep her love for Caelen burning bright and strong, but only she'd be aware of it.

As she walked along the walls of her keep, she prayed that Caelen would understand her dilemma and not hate her for her decision. But she would not blame him if he chose to hate her and despise her every day for the rest of his life. He had earned that right, she supposed, to hate her vehemently for breaking his heart and marrying another. If their roles were reversed she imagined she'd probably want to hate him if he married another.

She was almost to the keep when out of the corner of her eye, she spotted Bhruic as he made his way into the stables. That did not give her pause so much as the fact that Alyse followed him in only a moment later.

'Twasn't jealousy that made her veer away from the keep and toward the stables, but curiosity. She knew Alyse better than she knew Bhruic. Mayhap her instinct from the other night was correct, that Alyse had feelings for the man.

Ignoring the people she passed, Fiona made her way to the stables and peeked inside to mayhap catch a glimpse of her betrothed and his potential lover. Little bits of dust danced in the sunlight, the aroma of hay and horses filtered outside, but that was all that Fiona could make out. She looked up and down the stables but saw nothing but horses peering out over the doors. Straining her ears to listen, to hear over the occasional nicker or stomp of a hoof, she finally heard the low muffled voices coming from the stable master's private room to her right. The door stood slightly ajar, so she tiptoed toward it.

'Twas Bhruic and Alyse she heard, but their voices were low and muffled. Alyse was crying, but Fiona could only make out every few words. It sounded as though Bhruic was trying to comfort the poor woman.

"Wheesht, Alyse," Bhruic whispered.

Fiona could not hear what Alyse said next for her voice was so soft and low, but she could reason out that the woman was mightily heartbroken.

"I would change things," Bhruic whispered, then murmured something inaudible. "I have no choice … I love ye, Alyse, ye ken that …"

Fiona's heart suddenly felt quite constricted. Not once had she thought to ask Bhruic if there was another that he might love. She had not stopped to ask him what sacrifice he might be making. She'd only thought of all that she was giving up.

Unable to listen to the heartbreaking sobs coming from Alyse or Bhruic's attempts to console her, Fiona quietly slipped away.

Fiona did something she rarely did. She sought the counsel of her sisters-in-law. They had been in the kitchens, arguing with the cook over the meal he had planned for the wedding feast. She pulled the two women away with a lie that she wanted to try her gown on. Happily, they followed her above stairs and into her bedchamber. As soon as they were inside, Fiona bolted the door.

"I need to speak with ye," Fiona said. "But I need ye to promise ye'll no' say what ye *think* I want to hear, but rather what yer heart tells ye."

Isabelle and Mairi stared at her, perplexed, but nodded in silent agreement.

"Ye ken that I do no' love Bhruic," she began. "But I have just learned somethin'regardin' Bhruic and Alyse, that I fear changes everythin' about tomorrow."

Her sisters-in-law looked genuinely concerned, but waited for her to explain.

"I fear that Bhruic and Alyse love one another. Poor Alyse is heartbroken."

"Ye've talked to her?" Mairi asked.

Fiona shook her head, "Nay, but I've just overheard the two of them together, in the stables. Alyse was in tears, just a sobbin', and poor Bhruic sounded as though he wished to cry along with her. I've no doubt that they love each other."

Mairi and Isabelle glanced at one another, uncertain what it was exactly that Fiona wanted from them.

"I fear I've been verra selfish this past week," Fiona admitted as she wrapped her arms around her stomach. She felt ashamed of her own actions and complete lack of regard for the man she had pledged to marry. "No' once did I ask Bhruic what was in his heart. I've avoided him at every turn and I have been mopin' around and actin' like an arse."

From the expressions on her sisters-in-law faces they agreed wholeheartedly with her assessment.

"I do no' think I can marry Bhruic, not when I ken his heart belongs to Alyse. And what of Alyse? I marry the man she loves and she's forced to see the two of us together day after day?" She took a deep breath and let it out slowly. "I do no' want to enter into another marriage knowin' me husband canna or will no' ever care fer me. And I canna do that to him. 'Twould no' be fair to either of them, would it?"

Neither Isabelle nor Mairi had any answers for her.

"I fear 'twill be somethin' ye need to pray about, Fi," Isabelle said.

Prayer might be her last vestige of hope.

Fourteen

Fiona had done a good deal of soul-searching and praying the rest of the day. She could not in good conscience keep her word to marry Bhruic after she had discovered just how much he and Alyse loved each other. 'Twould have been a monumental mistake on her part to walk down that aisle and make an oath before God to love and honor a man who, not unlike herself, could not ever love her. At best, all they could hope for was a mutual friendship.

She knew the agony and suffering that Bhruic, and Alyse, would be forced to endure. Imagining herself in Alyse's shoes, watching the man she loved building a life with another woman was devastating. She simply could not do it.

After enlisting the aid of her sisters-in-law, it took very little effort to convince Alyse that it should be she who married Bhruic, not Fiona. They had pulled Alyse into Fiona's bedchamber after the evening meal and had an honest and heartfelt discussion on the matter.

Alyse, a sweet and bonny woman with blonde hair and big blue eyes, sat in a chair facing Fiona, Isabelle and Mairi. Sniffling and wiping away tears, she asked, "But what if Edgar refuses to allow it? What are we to do then?"

In truth, Fiona hadn't thought that far in advance. "We will think of somethin'," Fiona said, trying to sound more confident than she truly felt.

Alyse looked up at the women surrounding her. Fiona knew the young woman and mother of two small boys was doubtful. "If he does no' agree," Alyse began, "I will leave. I can go live with me mum's sister, she be a McLaren. I have already packed, ye see, because I did no' allow meself to hope fer a miracle."

Fiona could not rightly blame her. She would have done the same. "Do no' worry over it just yet," Fiona said as she glanced at Mairi and Isabelle. "Together, we'll think of a way fer ye to be with Bhruic, ye and all yer bairns together as a family, as it should be."

Mairi and Isabelle offered warm smiles to Alyse. "Aye," Isabelle said. "If anyone can convince a man to do a thing, 'twould be our Fiona."

Fiona wished she had as much faith in herself as her sister-in-law did.

'Twas just the two of them, Fiona and Edgar, sitting at the table in her private study. She had just informed him that she would not be marrying Bhruic on the morrow. To say Edgar MacKinnon was not a happy man would have been an understatement. Though he did not rant and rave or make threats, Fiona could see his fury simmering just under the surface.

"Ye made a promise," he said through gritted teeth.

"Aye, I did make a promise. But I canna in good conscience go to the altar on the morrow when I ken verra well that Bhruic loves another," Fiona told him.

His brow drew into a knot and looked as though he had not been party to that bit of information. Either Bhruic had not shared his feelings with his uncle or his uncle hadn't expected Fiona to find out.

"Alyse McPherson," Fiona gave him the name and waited for a reaction. A flicker of something menacing flashed behind Edgar's eyes. "She was a MacKinnon and married into our clan several years ago. Her husband was killed about the same time as my James died. She has two sons and had been verra good friends with Bhruic's wife. Since the deaths of their spouses, the two became good friends and that friendship turned into much more."

"I do no' see what that has to do with your promise to marry him. We had an agreement. Ye signed it. Ye made a promise. The weddin' be on the morrow." Though he was doing his best to maintain control, the sharp edge in his voice was unmistakable.

"The weddin' will still take place," Fiona said.

Edgar studied her for a moment, perplexed and angry all at

once.

"Bhruic will marry Alyse." She waited a few moments to allow him to mull it over. "I do no' expect ye to still offer yer warriors or anythin' else ye promised us. But I would still like us to be allies, Edgar. Ye and yers would always be welcome here. And the McPhersons will keep their word to offer ye aid should ye need it."

For inexplicable reasons, her promise that they would remain allies seemed to appease him. Clan MacKinnon was far bigger than the McPhersons. Why was it so important for them to remain allies? Mayhap it went along the lines of 'every little bit helps'. Aid, no matter how little or in what form, could eventually prove essential.

"What has Bhruic said on the matter?" Edgar asked, still keeping a suspicious eye on Fiona.

"I've no' yet discussed it with him. Out of respect of our friendship, I wanted to come to ye first. But I've seen the way Bhruic looks at Alyse. I doubt he'll be complainin' about a change in brides."

Edgar found that amusing and finally allowed himself to smile. "Me nephew be a romantic. I find it more an affliction than a blessin'." He took in a deep breath and seemed to ponder things for a moment. Finally, he gave a quick nod of his head. "Verra well then, Bhruic and Alyse may marry."

Relief washed over Fiona, but she managed to maintain her calm demeanor.

Edgar quickly added, "As long as ye promise we will remain allies."

"I do so promise," Fiona said.

"And I may visit often?"

Fiona raised a brow, uncertain why that was so important to him.

He grew uncomfortable under her close scrutiny. After a long, awkward silence, he said, "I was no' blessed with daughters, only sons. I've grown quite fond of Bhruic's wee daughter, Aingealag," he said as if he were ashamed to admit it. "And if ye e'r repeat that, I'll deny it!" he said, pointing a bony finger at her.

She had assumed that Bhruic would return to his own family after the wedding. "Ye intend for Bhruic to remain here?" she asked.

"Aye," Edgar said before quickly adding, "ye'll be needin' every able-bodied man ye can get."

That much was true. Still, she found it odd that Edgar would still insist Bhruic remain behind. Neither he nor Alyse were McPhersons.

"I'll no' be givin' ye the one hundred men I promised. But I can leave ye a few."

'Twas a most generous offer and she supposed she should not look a gift horse in the mouth. "Verra well then. I thank ye kindly, Edgar."

"And I may visit me grandniece?"

"Aye, ye may."

He looked much relieved and quite happy then. Why did some men feel ashamed at loving a person? Did they truly think it a sign of weakness? Resisting the urge to lecture him, she merely smiled. "So ye do possess a heart, after all." Fiona teased. He glared at her. "I give ye me word, I'll no' ever tell another livin' soul that ye have a heart, Edgar."

Fifteen

The next morning dawned bright and brilliant, with clear blue skies and not the slightest indication of rain. The McPherson keep was alive with excitement and anticipation, even if it was no longer their chief who was marrying Bhruic MacKinnon.

Fiona was truly happy for Alyse and Bhruic. Though she still hadn't solved the problem of the raids, she could be happy for the couple. She even went so far as to give over the beautiful blue gown that had been made for her, to Alyse. Isabelle and Mairi had stayed up late the night before, taking in the hem, waist and sleeves, so that it would fit the bride.

Though she would have liked to have gone through the entire day pretending she had not a care in the world, that was impossible. Until they were able to learn the identity of the men responsible for the raids, they would have to be even more cautious. Fiona ordered more men to the walls and more scouts to patrol their borders. Their resources were stretched thin enough as it was, but she could not afford to take any chances. The last thing they needed was to be caught unawares especially on this day.

Fiona had dressed for battle that morning, much to Mairi and Isabelle's vexation. "Certainly ye do no' plan to wear yer leather and mail to the weddin'?" Mairi asked while they broke their fast.

"I do," Fiona said, only because she took a good deal of pleasure in watching her sisters-in-law's looks of horror.

"Och! Fiona," Isabelle said. "Ye canna do that! 'Tis a special occasion! And ye be givin' the bride away!"

Unable to keep her expression serious any longer, Fiona burst into a fit of laughter. "Of course I'll no' be wearin' this!" She rolled her eyes at the two women. Teasing them even further and because she was well aware what the women thought of her auld, plain dresses, she said, "I'll wear me brown dress."

"That be even worse!" Mairi exclaimed.

Fiona rolled her eyes and smiled. "I ken now how me brothers were able to get such beautiful wives," she said. "Yer both gullible."

"Ye should no' tease like that," Isabelle chastised. "'Tis no' a nice thing to do."

"Please fergive me," Fiona said, unable to wipe away her smile. "I be in a verra fine mood this day." There was no denying that she felt very much like a convicted murderer who'd been given a pardon by the king.

Mairi nodded toward one of the tables below. "It appears as though Bhruic and Alyse be happy as well."

Alyse and her two sons sat at a table below, with Bhruic sitting across from them. They did look quite happy. Fiona had no doubt she had made the right decision, but something felt out of place at that table. It took a few moments before a sudden thought dawned. "Where be Bhruic's daughter?" She'd been so wrapped up in her own misery that she hadn't given any thought to the child.

Isabelle was adding jam to a slice of bread. "Alyse told me the child be ill. Nothin' too serious, but they felt it best to keep her at the MacKinnon keep. Edgar's family be takin' care of her."

"I hope it be nothin' serious," Fiona said with growing concern. If it were her child who was ill, she imagined wild horses could not have dragged her away from the child's side. Mayhap 'twas different for fathers.

"Nay," Isabelle said. "Nothin' serious from what I be told. They'll send the child here as soon as she is better."

Collin entered the gathering room, wee Symon in his arms. They made their way to the dais, where Symon reached out for his mum. Mairi's eyes always lit with love whenever her husband or her son were near. For once, Fiona felt no jealousy at the sight, just happiness for her brother and his family.

After handing Symon off to Mairi, Collin sat down between his wife and sister. "The MacKinnon offered some of his men to help with patrols this day," he said as he stabbed at a piece of ham and placed it on his trencher. "I say he's takin' the change in brides quite well."

"Aye, he is," Fiona said as she finished the last bite of her eggs. "He wants us to remain allies, though I must admit I do no' ken why."

"Mayhap it be yer sweet disposition," Collin quipped.

Fiona laughed at his jest. "That *must* be it."

"I must agree, I wonder the same," Collin said as he glanced around the busy room. "But fer now, I be glad to have the extra help, and even more relieved yer sudden change in heart did no' start a clan war."

Fiona took a sideways glance at her brother. She could not fault him for his honesty for she had been worried over that as well. Edgar MacKinnon however, had proved to be a just man, a man with a heart at least where his grandniece was concerned.

"Have we had any word from Brodie?" Fiona asked.

Collin nodded. "He sent word a few days ago that he'd no' miss yer weddin' fer all the world. I did send word this mornin' that there was a change in plans. 'Twill be later this day before our messengers return."

Fiona missed her brother. He had sent word more than a week ago, that his wounds were healing nicely, though he hated laying abed all day. She was glad he would be returning for she missed his councel and cheery disposition.

"I be glad to hear it, Collin. There be a level of mischievousness missin' from our keep these past weeks that only Brodie can fill."

Collin chuckled and stuffed eggs into his mouth. "True," he said.

Done eating, Fiona pushed away from the table. "I want to check the walls again," she told Collin. When he started to stand, she placed a hand on his shoulder. "Nay, finish eatin', brother. I will no' be gone long." She looked to Isabelle and Mairi. "Will ye be so kind as to meet me in me bedchamber after the noonin' meal? I fear I canna get into me green dress without yer aid."

Their eyes lit with relief and glee. "Aye, we can," Mairi said as she gave Symon a bit of bread.

Kissing the top of Symon's head, she bid them all a good morn.

After patrolling the walls, Fiona met with their smithy and

weapons maker. She was pleased to see that he'd been stockpiling enough arrows that they could withstand a year-long assault.

Feeling better than she had in a long time, she made another walk along the walls before heading to the bathhouse. Sufficiently scrubbed from head to toe, she stepped into a robe, gathered her belongings and went to her bed chamber. She had passed by Mairi's room, where she and Isabelle were helping Alyse ready herself for her wedding. Alyse's smile lit the room.

"We'll be along to help ye soon," Isabelle promised as she held up the dress that had been meant for Fiona. 'Twas a beautiful blue gown, the color of the sky on a sunny day. Made of fine blue silk, the hem and sleeves were trimmed in gold threads. Alyse would look stunning in it.

"Do no' worry," Fiona said. "The bride first."

Leaving them to fuss over Alyse, Fiona went to her room and shut the door.

The hearth was cold, so she built a new fire. Once it caught, she pulled the stool up and sat near it, thankful for the warmth, as well as some time to be alone with her own thoughts.

She thought back to what Collin had said about Brodie's message. Nothing was mentioned of Caelen or his reaction to the news that she was to have been married this day. Admittedly, she was a bit hurt that Caelen hadn't come storming down her walls when the banns were read. Mayhap he did not love her as much as she thought he had.

'Twas also possible that he had been so overcome and grief-stricken that he was left paralyzed with sadness. Even she had to scoff at that idea. Nay, the Caelen she knew would have come to fight for her.

Why hadn't he? Not so much as a letter of good wishes for her. Nothing. Mayhap he was so angry that it had taken Phillip, Kenneth and ten men to tie him up and lock him in the dungeon until after the wedding. She could just imagine Kenneth suggesting it. She knew he did not like her much and keeping Caelen locked away until after the wedding, until nothing could be done about it, was just the sort of thing he would do.

In the end, it didn't really matter. She wasn't marrying Bhruic. And there was no way she could be with Caelen.

Still, it would have been nice had the man she loved shown

some sign, a small gesture of some sort that he objected to her marrying another man.

Combing her hair out with her fingers, she cursed under her breath. "What did ye expect, Fiona? Ye broke the poor man's heart, and yer own in the process. Do ye really think he'd come runnin' just to have ye break it again?" Nay, not even Caelen McDunnah was that tetched.

Sixteen

Caelen had never shown any animal such disregard as he did now. Tearing across the Highlands at breakneck speed, he was determined to stop Fiona from marrying. Pushing his mount beyond its limits, its sleek coat slathered in foam as Caelen urged it on further.

Hours away from Fiona's keep, Brodie pulled up alongside him. "Caelen, ye'll kill that fine horse if ye do no' slow down. Then I fear, I'll have to kill ye fer showin' it no mercy."

Caelen pulled back slightly, knowing Brodie was right. Like a berzerker determined to fulfill his quest, 'twas difficult for Caelen to remain calm. If he judged the time correctly, he was going to miss his one and only opportunity to keep Fiona from marrying this man named Bhruic.

"Phillip be there, Caelen," Brodie said for what seemed the hundredth time. "He has strict orders to take whatever measures are necessary to keep Fiona from the altar."

For Phillip's sake, he hoped Brodie was right. For if he did not arrive in time, and Phillip hadn't been able to delay the wedding, Caelen would be left with no choice but to kill him.

Isabelle and Mairi looked quite proud of their accomplishments. "Ye look beautiful, Fiona!" Mairi exclaimed.

Dressed in the beautiful green gown, with the McPherson plaid draped across her shoulder, her hair combed and styled in curls and ringlets, Fiona never felt more out of place or at unease. She fidgeted with the bodice, pulling it up and tucking her breasts in, she felt half-naked. "Yer cruel women, ye ken that, don't ye?" she said as she continued to make attempts to cover her bare skin.

"Ye look beautiful," Mairi said, ignoring Fiona's complaints.

"But I be no' the one marryin' this day," Fiona told them as she reached for her belt and sword.

"Nay!" Isabelle said as she grabbed the sword from Fiona's grasp. "Ye canna go to the church as if ye were armed for battle."

Fiona rolled her eyes. "Were it a *man* givin' Alyse away, ye'd no' argue him donnin' his sword."

"But ye already have yer *sgian dubhs* hidden under the dress and in the sleeves," Mairi argued.

Fiona twisted the sword out of Isabelle's hands. "Aye, I have me *sgian dubhs* and I'll wear me sword. I'll no' argue it further."

Mairi let out a frustrated breath and threw her hands up in defeat. "Verra well then, Fiona."

Fiona wrapped the leather belt around her waist then draped the length of plaid over the sword. "See? Ye can barely see it," she told her sisters-in-law.

"I do no' see why ye feel the need to arm yerself. 'Tis a weddin' for heaven's sake," Isabelle said.

"Aye, 'tis a weddin' and the kirk will be filled with all manner of people. Some of whom might wish to do us harm. I'll no' pretend all is well and go anywhere unarmed."

Isabelle and Mairi, though not happy that she had insisted on arming herself to the teeth, could not blame her for wanting to be cautious. If the past weeks had proved anything, it was that they should not be caught with their arms down.

"Now," Fiona said as she clapped her hands together. "What say we go get Alyse and Bhruic married."

"I should no' have let ye talk me in to fresh horses!" Caelen cursed at Kenneth and Brodie. "We wasted valuable time!"

They had stopped in a village just a few hours east of McPherson lands for fresh horses. In truth, it really hadn't taken them that far out of the way, but Caelen was too angry and too determined to listen to reason.

"Aye, and if we hadn't," Kenneth began, "ye'd have ended up havin' to walk all the way to Brodie's keep."

He knew it was true, but at the moment, he did not care. His sole and only focus was to get to the McPherson keep and stop this bloody wedding.

What on earth had possessed Fiona to agree to marry this MacKinnon? It could not be love, of that he was certain. Nay, she must be marrying under duress. Mayhap someone had kidnapped one of her brothers or sisters-in-law, or worse yet, her wee nephew, and the only way to secure their safety was to agree to marry. He had convinced himself 'twas the only thing that made a bit of sense.

He would go to her, demand an explanation, and help her with whatever mess she was in. He would accept nothing less than the full truth. No matter how she would protest that she could take care of her own problems, he would insist on helping her. Even if it meant tying her to her bed, or locking her away in their oubliette. He was too angry to be above anything so harsh as locking her away.

He would do whatever he must in order to ensure her safety.

Seventeen

Alyse looked stunning in her blue gown and the gossamer veil affixed to her beautiful blonde locks. Fiona stood beside her, holding her hand as they descended the stairs to the gathering room. Isabelle and William were waiting below, with Alyse's young sons.

"Mum!" her five-year-old son squealed with delight when he saw her. "Ye look pretty!"

Alyse beamed at her boys who came running up to hug her. "Careful, now," she said. "The dress be no' mine. We do no' want to ruin it."

The boys stepped away and apologized. "No worries, lads," Fiona told them. "Are ye ready to lead us to the kirk?"

The boys nodded excitedly and took their positions in front of Fiona and Alyse. "Verra good, lads," Fiona praised them for standing so tall and proud. "Now remember, do no' go too fast."

William and Isabelle came over and stood in front of the boys. "Are we ready?" William asked with a glance first to Alyse and then to Fiona.

"I believe so," Alyse said, her eyes beginning to fill with tears of joy. She whispered to Fiona, "I canna believe this is truly happenin'!"

Fiona gave her hand a gentle squeeze before nodding at William to begin their procession to the kirk.

Their tiny kirk was filled to capacity. People lined the walls and spilled out into the yard, to watch Alyse and Bhruic marry. Fiona felt quite certain that none cared too much who was being married today, for the celebration was going to be grand either way.

To date, she had seen five brides down the aisle since assuming the role of chief. But this was the first time for a ceremony or celebration of this grandeur. Typically, 'twas just her clan in attendance, and the kirk was big enough to hold anyone who wanted to attend.

But with four other chiefs and their people in attendance this day, the kirk couldn't hold them all. Still, it was a momentous and happy occasion.

William and Isabelle led the way down the aisle to the altar. Bhruic was waiting, a proud smile painted on his face. Father Thomas, an aulder priest from a neighboring village was here to officiate. He waited for William and Isabelle to make their way toward the front, before giving a slight nod for the two boys to begin.

Fiona was happy for this little family, for the bride she was going to give away in just a few short moments. She refused to be jealous or to think of Caelen and what might have been between them. This was Alyse and Bhruic's day, not hers.

As soon as the boys were at the altar, standing next to Isabelle, Fiona began to lead Alyse down. "Yer certain ye want to marry that man?" Fiona whispered, tongue in cheek.

Alyse smiled, unable to take her eyes from Bhruic. "Aye, I be certain."

Fiona gave her hand another gentle squeeze and soon, they were standing before the priest. The auld man, looked out at the overflowing kirk and smiled. "Ye may be seated."

A quiet rustling of people taking their seats fell over the kirk. Somewhere near the back, Fiona could hear wee Symon cooing and making noises, quickly followed by Mairi quietly shushing him.

"We are gathered here today," the priest began in a loud voice that belied his small stature. "To celebrate and bless the union between Bhruic MacKinnon and Alyse McPherson. 'Tis a momentous and joyous occasion, one that should not be entered into lightly."

Fiona glanced at Bhruic who looked as proud as a peacock, wearing his best tunic, trews and MacKinnon plaid. He could not take his eyes from his bride. For a brief moment, Fiona felt a pang of remorse, for he looked at Alyse the way Caelen had once looked at her.

The priest asked everyone to bow their heads as he said a blessing over the couple. When he finished, he looked at Fiona and asked, "Who gives this bride to Bhruic today?"

Before Fiona could utter a single word, a shout came out from behind her.

"No one gives away the bride!"

Fiona cringed as she heard heavy footsteps stomping down the aisle. 'Twas Caelen. *He picked a fine bloody time to show up!* She cursed before turning around to look at him.

He was furious. His face was purple with rage, his eyes fine slits, his jaw clenching as he stomped toward the altar. *Well,* she thought, *that answers the question on how he felt about me marryin' Bhruic.*

Before she could utter a word, Caelen was standing between her and the groom. If looks could kill, Bhruic would have burst into flames from the furious glare Caelen was giving him. Poor Bhruic looked quite confused.

"Caelen, what are ye doin' here?" Fiona whispered harshly.

"I've come to stop ye from makin' the biggest mistake of yer life," he ground out as he continued to stare at Bhruic.

"Fiona, who is this?" Bhruic asked.

Caelen gave her no time to answer. "I take it ye be the groom?"

Bhruic nodded as his eyes darted between Fiona and Caelen.

"The only reason ye still breathe, MacKinnon, is because we be in a kirk. I suggest ye keep yer mouth shut."

"Good lord, Caelen," Fiona said. "I will speak to ye after the ceremony, now go!"

"No' bloody likely," Caelen said before picking Fiona up and tossing her over his shoulder.

In the blink of an eye, Fiona could hear swords being drawn from all quarters. "Caelen, put me down ye fool!" she yelled as he stomped toward the exit.

"No' bloody likely."

She pounded a fist against his back as he came to an abrupt halt.

She could not see what or who it was that stopped his forward progression. "Out of me way, Collin," Caelen ground out.

"I do no' think so," Collin answered. Fiona didn't need to see her brother, to know he was blocking the way out, probably with his sword drawn and murder in his eyes. She lifted herself up, placing her hands on Caelen's shoulders. She could see all the swords glinting in the afternoon light, the murderous expressions on countless faces. She sighed and said, "Hold!" before anyone made an attempt to kill Caelen.

As best as she could, she turned slightly, still unable to see Collin. "Brother, he'll no' hurt me, step out of the way so that I might speak with the bloody eejit!"

A long moment passed before she heard Collin step away. Caelen thundered out of the kirk and headed across the yard. People from within the kirk spilled out, mouths agape, uncertain what, if anything they should do.

"I will be fine!" she reassured them. She was not at all fearful of Caelen. He would do nothing to harm her. And even though she was quite glad for his foolish display, it irked her to no end that he would not listen to her command to be set down.

"Caelen, put me down so we can discuss this like two mature intelligent adults."

Before she knew it, she was being unceremoniously tossed off his shoulder and handed up and onto the back of a horse, that also happened to be occupied by Kenneth. "Fergive me, Fiona," Kenneth said as he took a tight hold of her waist.

"Caelen McDunnah!" she shouted after him. He was stomping toward his own horse. Surrounding her were several McDunnah men on horseback, and her brother Brodie. Confusion and anger set it.

"Caelen McDunnah! I demand that ye put a halt to this nonsense at once!" She yelled across the yard at him. He mounted, spun his horse around and called back to her, "No' bloody likely."

Prologe to A Breath of Promise

"Are ye armed?" Phillip asked as he wrapped an arm around her waist and tapped the flanks of his horse.

Fiona turned her head slightly to look him in the eye. "I be *always* armed," she reminded him, her words clipped and sharp. Her sword was within reach. One *sgian dubh* was carefully hidden in her left sleeve while two more were strapped to her thighs. Though she could very well have threatened Phillip with his life if he didn't stop and let her down, the person toward whom she really wished to vent her anger was riding ahead of them.

"Can I have yer word ye will no' gut me?" he asked as they galloped across the yard.

"I may no' gut *ye,* but as fer Caelen?" Nay, she couldn't make that promise.

"I be sorry fer this, Fiona," Phillip said. He did sound remorseful as well as a wee fearful. They were racing toward the gate.

"He loves ye, Fiona. Ye canna gut a man that loves ye."

She might not gut him completely, but she couldn't necessarily promise she wouldn't make a few pointed cuts here and there.

"Where are ye takin' me?" she demanded.

Phillip remained silent as they followed Caelen, Brodie and a dozen other men through the gate. Another dozen McDunnah men brought up the rear. The ground thundered with the reverberation of dozens of horses galloping across the land.

"Has he lost his mind?" Fiona asked through gritted teeth.

"Aye, I be afraid he has."

She continued to seethe while she watched Caelen tear across the countryside like a madman. *When I get me hands on that man...* Though she could not blame Caelen for being angry, that was no reason for him to kidnap her like this. 'Twas too ridiculous for words. 'Twas all anyone needed to prove the man was completely and unequivocally insane. Just what he thought to gain by this act of madness was beyond her.

"Where on earth are we goin'?" she asked, growing angrier and angrier.

Phillip turned mute again and urging their mount to go faster. The farther they rode from her keep the more infuriated she became. She already knew Caelen loved her and he knew that she knew. What then was the purpose of interrupting the wedding ceremony and stealing her away like this? Several long moments passed and she began to realize they were heading for McDunnah lands. More likely than not, Caelen's keep.

No' bloody likely.

Carefully, Fiona removed the *sgian dubh* from her sleeve. Once she had a firm grip on it, she slowly turned as best she could to face Phillip. "Ye will stop this horse at once."

Phillip ignored her.

"I give ye one more chance, Phillip," she warned him as she placed the blade of the *sgian dubh* against his throat.

"Bloody hell," he murmured. "Put that away."

"No' bloody likely," she smiled up at him. "Stop this horse *now.*"

Phillip's nostrils flared as his face turned red with anger. A moment later, he pulled rein. "He will kill me fer this."

Fiona knew as well as Phillip did that Caelen wouldn't truly take his life. Once the horse came to a halt, Fiona tossed her leg over and slid down. Phillip followed her.

The men who had been following them pulled up as well, all of them looking utterly baffled. One of them asked, "Why did ye stop?" Before Phillip could answer, the young man spotted the *sgian dubh* in Fiona's hand.

"Ye didna search her first?" he asked.

Phillip rolled his eyes. "Would *ye* like to search her?" he ground out. The color left the young man's face. "What should we do?"

Phillip raked a hand across his face as he watched Fiona begin to pace back and forth. "We wait until our insane chief realizes we have stopped."

The men remained mounted and they, too, began to watch Fiona pace back and forth.

They had travelled far enough that she could barely make out her keep in the distance. 'Twas not too far a distance to walk if she had to. In the opposite direction, Caelen and the others were still heading toward McDunnah lands. She stopped pacing and turned to face Phillip. "What on earth possessed him to do this?"

Phillip's face bore the expression of a man thin on patience. "To stop ye from marryin'. I tried to get into the keep to talk to ye' but they would no' let me in."

Fiona scoffed at his remark. "By 'talk' ye mean delay the weddin' until he could get here?"

He made no attempt to lie. "Aye, to do just that."

She muttered a curse under her breath. None of them had been made aware of the change in brides. That knowledge helped assuage some of her anger, but not all of it. Taking a deep breath she let it out slowly. "I was no' marryin' Bhruic."

Phillip raised a doubtful brow. "Ye were at the altar."

"Aye, but I was no' the bride. I was givin' the bride away."

His doubtful brow fell, his confusion quite evident. "What?"

"That be right," she said as understanding began to spread across his face. "Yer foolish, tetched, pigheaded leader did no' stop me from marryin' this day. I was merely givin' the bride away."

"But the banns were posted," Phillip mumbled.

"And I changed me mind."

"But why?" he stammered as he tried to make sense of it.

There were many reasons why she had chosen not to marry Bhruic. But she'd be damned to hell for eternity before she shared them with Phillip.

The sound of hoof beats heading toward them drew her attention. 'Twas Caelen. He'd finally realized they were no longer behind them.

"Phillip," Fiona said as she took one step back. "I would greatly appreciate it if ye'd allow me to explain everythin' to Caelen."

Phillip needed no coaxing on the matter.

As Caelen drew nearer Fiona could see the fury in his eyes. He didn't even wait for his horse to come to a complete stop before he slid down and thundered toward her.

Fiona drew her sword. "Halt!" she demanded.

"We'll no' be playin' games this day, Fiona," he warned. He stopped with the tip of her sword touching his chest. "I be no' in the mood fer it."

"Ye will stop actin' like a fool and listen to me, Caelen McDunnah."

There was no denying his fury. His brown eyes were so dark they were nearly black, his face as red as a beet, and the vein in his neck throbbed as fast as her heart was beating against her chest.

She spied Brodie then. "I see ye can ride again, brother."

Brodie cleared his throat and looked like a child caught stealing sweet cakes. "Do no' kill him, Fi," he said.

"I'll no kill him if he agrees that we will discuss this like two, intelligent adults," she said, directing her statement directly at Caelen. "No more tossin' me on a horse and carryin' me away. Do ye understand?"

His nostrils flared and his eyes turned to slits.

"Why were ye goin' to marry that MacKinnon?" he asked. His voice was low, almost a growl. The men around them began to scatter, to give them their privacy. Fiona noted, however, that they did not go far. They probably worried that she would gut him if provoked.

"We were attacked again. This time they killed a man and his wife and left their two young children orphans," she told him. "I had verra few options."

"I would have protected ye," he growled.

"By marryin' Bhruic, I could remain chief and gain one hundred MacKinnon men, fightin' men and Clan MacKinnon as our ally. Clan McPherson would remain Clan McPherson," she told him.

She didn't think it possible, but he grew even angrier. "I could have given ye ten times that many men," he said through gritted teeth.

'Twas a conversation they had had before. Her head began to pound from the frustration. "Aye, and Clan McPherson would have been lost and I would have broken me vows and me oath." Why was it so difficult for him to understand?

"I love ye, Fiona. Why can ye no' see that?" he asked, his voice sounding less harsh and angry. Instead he sounded like a man in pain.

"I ken that ye love me," she said in a soft voice. "And ye ken that I love ye. But I had no other choices, Caelen."

Her train of thought was interrupted by the sound of horses. Fiona turned to see William, Collin and five of her men rapidly approaching. As she waited, she pondered on whether or not she should tell Caelen the truth— that she wasn't the bride this day. Turning around, she saw the pain and anger in his eyes. She hadn't meant for any of this to happen, to hurt him. She was about to confess when he stepped forward.

"Ye love bein' chief more than ye love me," he said with an accusatory tone, the anger returning again.

His accusation infuriated her, causing her good will to evaporate in the blink of an eye. How dare he suggest such a thing? "Would ye have given up bein' chief to be with me? Would ye have allowed Clan McDunnah to become Clan McPherson?"

His expression told her that he thought her quite mad to even suggest such a thing. It stung. Why should she be the one to make all the sacrifices so they could be together?

"Ye can take yer accusation and stick it up —"

Collin called out her name as he and the others pulled their horses to a stop.

"Caelen!" Collin said as he approached. "I be glad to see she has no' killed ye."

I be about to do just that, Fiona fumed silently as she stared at Caelen.

"Fiona, 'tis done," Collin said as he stood next to her.

Before she could utter a word, Caelen asked, "What be done?"

"The weddin'," Collin said with a smile. "Bhruic and Alyse be married now."

A tumult of emotions flashed across Caelen's face. Confusion turned to understanding and then to sheer unadulterated anger, then to something she could not quite describe. All she knew was that she should probably protect herself.

Before she could raise her sword again, Caelen grabbed her wrist. "When were ye plannin' on tellin' me that?"

Suddenly she felt quite certain that this must be what a rabbit feels like when caught in a snare. She stammered for a few moments before she managed to say, "I was gettin' to that when ye accused me of lovin' bein' chief more than lovin' ye."

He cocked his head to one side and studied her closely. All at once she began to feel quite uncomfortable under such close scrutiny.

"So ye be no' marryin' this day?" he asked.

Straightening her shoulders and lifting her chin, she replied, "This day? Nay, no' this day."

Caelen took one step closer, refusing to let go of her wrist. "Why did ye no' marry him?"

There were too many eyes upon her to answer as honestly as either of them would have liked. "I had me reasons."

"Fiona, why did ye no' marry him?" he asked again in a much lower voice, but it was still quite demanding.

"I had me reasons and that be all ye need to ken at the moment, Caelen McDunnah," she told him.

William's deep growl of frustration startled her. She had not heard him dismount or approach and now he was standing behind her. "Ye both are tetched!"

Taking advantage of the opportunity his distraction offered, Fiona freed herself from Caelen's grasp.

"I be nowhere near as tetched as he is," Fiona said with a nod toward Caelen.

William rolled his eyes and shook his head. "As far as I be concerned yer both tetched and deservin' of each other. I do no' see why do ye no' just marry him."

Now who is tetched? she thought as she looked at her brother. "I canna break me vows or oaths," she reminded him. "I canna allow Clan McPherson to fall."

"It does no' have to fall," William said.

"If I marry Caelen, our clan will be absorbed into his." She began to wonder why she'd ever thought of William as the more intelligent of her three brothers.

"Only if yer chief," William said. His eyes went from Fiona to Caelen then back to Fiona. She was at a loss as to what he was thinking.

William took a deep breath and let it out in a whoosh of frustration. "Fiona, if ye were to die on the morrow, what happens?"

She was completely lost and not tracking his line of thinking.

"Who becomes chief?" William asked, hopeful that she'd finally follow his line of thinking.

"Collin," she answered, still uncertain what this had to do with anything.

"Right!" he said happily.

"I do no' ken what yer gettin' at, William," she told him.

William shook his head again. "If ye were no' chief, would ye marry Caelen?"

She didn't want to answer *too* quickly for she didn't want Caelen's head to get too big for his shoulders. "Possibly."

Caelen grunted his disproval of her answer. He mumbled something that sounded remarkably similar to 'liar'.

"Ye would marry him," William said. "And if ye were to die tomorrow, Collin becomes chief."

Collin seemed to understand suddenly where his brother was going. "William, are ye suggestin' Fiona give up the chiefdom?"

A smile erupted on William's face. "Exactly!"

'Twas then that clarity dawned. Was William serious? Was he truly suggesting that she give up the chiefdom, hand it all over to Collin, so that she could marry Caelen? Her mind reeled and she began to feel lightheaded.

"Well?" Caelen chose that moment to speak.

Fiona's eyes flittered between her brothers and Caelen.

Could she really do that? Give up her position as chief to marry the slightly tetched man with the hopeful expression written on his face?

Oh good Lord.

About The Author

Note: This is the long story of how I became a full-time author. Normally, these things are only one or two paragraphs long. So many people have asked that I decided to add this information to my books.

I've been writing since childhood. Everything from short stories, full length novels, screenplays and even dabbled at poetry. I wrote because I loved it and it was also a means of escaping. I was horribly, painfully introverted. My stories allowed me to be whoever I wanted to be.

My secret dream was to be an author, but I never thought it would be possible. I knew how hard it was to 'get published' so I didn't even bother to submit any of my work to a traditional publishing house.

It was an accidental journey to becoming a full time, published author. I tell people that I didn't do it on purpose, even though it was a lifelong dream.

It started out as a whim of sorts. I wanted to give my mother a Kindle for her birthday. I thought it would be a hoot if when she turned the Kindle on for the first time, the first book she saw would be something I had written. And so it began.

I would get up at 3:30 every morning just to write. At the time, we only had one computer in the house so very early morning hours were my only opportunity to write. My husband thought I was getting up early to play Farmville!

I shared a few chapters with a very dear friend of mine, thinking she'd say "Cute. But don't give up your day job." I was floored when she emailed me back and said, "Where is the rest of it?? I want to read more!" I thought she was just being nice.

Somewhere along the way, my husband had discovered my little book on the computer. I had to come clean and explain to him what I was doing. I also asked him for help. I'm not a technical person,

Suzan Tisdale

but I figured there had to be a way to do get my book onto Mamma's Kindle. Now, anyone who knows my husband knows what a research nut he is. Give him the most obscure or offbeat or technical idea or question and he'll research the heck out of it! I had explained to him that I had seen a link at Amazon that said "Publish Your Book To Kindle", but that I hadn't bothered with it. I was convinced that all I needed was a 'cord' of some sort to hook up between my computer and Mamma's Kindle.

A few days later, my husband informed me that I couldn't just put my book on mom's Kindle. I had to actually publish it. I believed him. He's smart, this husband of mine and he'd never lied to me before.

I figured what the heck, go for it. What did I have to lose? No one would want to buy my book anyway. Now, deep down I had a secret desire to actually sell a copy, but I wouldn't speak the words out loud. I thought it would be wonderful if I sold just ten little copies. In my lifetime. Ten. That was a good goal.

Without the aid of an editor or cover artist and not having a clue what I was doing, I decided to go for it. I figured that I didn't want to wake up on my 60th birthday and wonder what if.... So In December of 2011 I published Laiden's Daughter.

By February of 2012, it was number 2 on Amazon's Top 100 Best Seller's List! Blew. My. Mind. I thought it would take a lifetime to sell ten copies. I was certain it had to be a mistake of some kind. But when I started getting one message after another, one positive review after another, I realized it wasn't a mistake....I was now an author.

I was selling more than 250 copies a day! I didn't have a clue what that meant, if in fact it meant anything at all. All that I knew was that I was over-the-moon happy and people were asking for more!

I remember my first royalty check from Amazon/KDP. $78.69. I cried because I felt like I had arrived. By October of 2012, I was able to give up my day job (selling insurance) in order to write full time. That still blows my mind. I am able to do things now that would not have been possible prior to December of 2011. I have the most amazing life.

In all honesty, it has never been about the money, its always been about the writing. Are my books perfection personified? Hardly. But I do know that my writing gets better with each new book -- and that is how it should be. I want to write stories that people will enjoy. I want to help people escape the ordinary, for just a little while.

Now, I have a beautiful editor, a very talented cover artist, and other indie authors who are very dear friends. I even have a street team! Suzan's Highland Lassies. This is a group of beautiful, sweet and smart women who I consider dear friends. I couldn't get through a book launching without them!

I also believe I have the most beautiful readers anywhere. I know that I would not be where I am today if it were not for them.

So there you have it. I'm proof that dreams can come true and that happily-ever-afters are real.

About the Author (Condensed)

Suzan lives in the Midwest with her verra handsome husband and the youngest of their four children. They are currently seeking monetary donations to help feed their 17- year-old, 6' 3" built-like-a-linebacker son.

"There is great joy in writing, but an even greater joy in sharing what you've written." —Suzan Tisdale

Stay Up To Date:
www.suzantisdale.com
www.facebook/suzantisdaleromance.com
Twitter: @suzantisdale
email: suzan@suzantisdale.com

Other Books by Suzan Tisdale

<u>The Clan MacDougall Series</u>

Laiden's Daughter

Findley's Lass

Wee William's Woman

McKenna's Honor

<u>The Clan Graham Series</u>

Rowan's Lady

Frederick's Queen

<u>The Clan McDunnah Series</u>

Caelen's Wife - A Trilogy- Book One: A Murmur of Providence

Caelen's Wife - Book Two - A Whisper of Fate

Caelen's Wife - Book Three - A Breath of Promise - March 2015

<u>Moirra's Heart Series</u>

Stealing Moirra's Heart - Part of *The Highland Winds Collection*

Saving Moirra's Heart - arriving 2015

Made in the USA
Lexington, KY
21 September 2015